DATE DUE

DEMCO

ASHES
IN
THE
RAIN

ASHES
IN
THE
RAIN

Selected Essays

AL MARTINEZ

ASHES IN THE RAIN
A TQS Book/Published by arrangement with the Los Angeles Times.

First Printing: March 1989

Library of Congress Cataloging-in-Publication Data
Martinez, Al.
Ashes in the rain : selected essays
I. Title.
PS3563.A7333A9   1989   814'.54   89-4400
ISBN: 0-89229-019-6 (pbk)

TQS Books are published by TQS Publications, a division of
Tonatiuh-Quinto Sol International, Inc.

TQS PUBLICATIONS
Post Office Box 9275
Berkeley, California 94709

PRINTED IN THE UNITED STATES OF AMERICA

10   9   8   7   6   5   4   3   2   1

Dedication

As Always,

For Joanne and our Gang of Eight.

And for anyone who has ever laughed

when I've wanted them to.

Introduction

This is the time of the Santa Ana winds in Los Angeles, and even as I write they blow in capricious gusts outside my window, whipping the last of the crimson gold leaves from the liquid amber trees and snapping dead branches from the giant oaks.

Fortunately, it has also been a time of rain or we would be tuned to the sound of sirens and the first whiffs of smoke in the mountains that surround us, because the Santa Anas can combine with intense drought conditions to create a dangerous alliance.

But while we are spared that coalition of wind and drought, we were not spared a deeper act of nature just before dawn today when an earthquake of moderate severity shook and rumbled Southern California awake and caused us to reflect on the fragile nature of our being on a planet continually under nature's siege.

I mention these phenomena because fires and earthquakes create the proper perspective in which to view the human institutions I often write about, and because they provide an explanation for the title of this book, *"Ashes in the Rain."*

We are an entertaining if not always rational species and our follies cry out for comment. We celebrate fools and suffer genius to mockery. We build statues of glory to battles that kill us. We drink poison to create profit and blacken the air we breathe with chemicals to enhance life styles.

But, still, there is redemption in chaos, and even as we smother ourselves with toxics that blind our vision, voices rise that caution temperance, that urge atonement, that sing of life's sweetness in growing crescendo around the arc of the Earth.

We don't have to die in our own fires, they tell us. Nature provides for its own regeneration. The story of resurrection is rooted in the springtime of rebirth.

Never has this been clearer to me than on a rainy March day three years ago when I hiked over hills that five months earlier had been ravaged by brush fires burning from the San Fernando Valley to the sea. Flames turned the terrain into a disordered moonscape of scorched earth and blackened trees, and I thought nothing would ever grow there again. I had not reckoned with nature.

I could not believe what I saw on that rainy day in March less than half a year later. What had once been fire's devastation was now a celebration of nature: wildflowers of every hue and color pushing up through the damp ashes to glow in the storm light in an affirmation of life I may never see again.

I wrote about them in a column, included herein, called *"Ashes in the Rain,"* and I repeat that title for this book, because I think that what I am in the long run is not so much a chronicler of woe or a satirist defining human folly as a messenger of redemption who believes that in the wake of every calamity, spring will come again.

Al Martinez
Topanga, California

CONTENTS

PEOPLE

FAMILY

ISSUES

ETHNIC

HUMOR

NATURE

NOSTALGIA
AND OBSERVATIONS

PEOPLE

No
Sad Songs
For Us

We would tolerate the
wounds we inflicted
on each other, because
ours was the combat
of young lions....

I awoke early the day my best friend died, and I don't know why. I sat out on the deck and watched a pale dawn wash through the sky, heavy with a fog that lingered in the mountains and dripped from the oak trees.

It wasn't until later that his wife called to tell me that Jerry Belcher had let go the pain and fear that accompanies cancer, and cold silence lay where an immense energy had burned.

He was the Nick I wrote about when he was told two months ago that he was going to die, so it was no surprise when the end came.

I saw him for the last time a week ago, a gaunt and skeletal man on a rented hospital bed in the living room of his home, barely able to talk, but still able to peer at me closely and whisper, "Where in the hell did you get that jacket?"

It was an affirmation of our ties: a friendship rooted in combat, bound in steel and tested each time we were together, even the last time.

I took his hand and sat next to him and we just looked at each other, half-smiling. Then I said it was a Penney's Outlet sale jacket and he said, "I thought so."

I didn't cry and he didn't cry, because that's not what our bond was. We had truth between us, and truth is closer and deeper and stronger than tears.

No sad songs for us, my friend.

Belcher was my confidant, my competitor and my critic for 30 years, with a wit like the sting of a wasp, and 10,000 times we battled over trivialities elevated to supremacy in a wash of dry martinis.

These were no casual debates. We clashed over who was fastest and who was best and once even over who *wasn't* best, for reasons lost in the blurry past.

I argued that his command of words far surpassed mine, and he argued that my style of prose towered over his, and to prove it we decided on a write-off.

4

We stalked through the rain from a bar called the Hollow Leg toward the city room of the Oakland Tribune across the street.

But halfway there we realized that, in order to prove the point, we would have to leave the judging to others, and that was an intrusion neither of us could abide, so we returned to the Hollow Leg and called it a tie and toasted the storm.

We could tolerate the wounds we inflicted on each other, because ours was the combat of young lions in the process of maturing, but we knew better than to seek judgment from those who could not begin to fathom our truths.

They were good days. We drank too much, but by God we *communicated*, and that's rare between warriors.

The Hollow Leg was our special place, and whoever wrote slowest on a given day would have to holler "Save me a place at the bar!" as the other headed out the door.

It was a shout of concession, but only for today. There was always tomorrow.

When I came to L.A., Belch followed a couple of years later. But he was never really happy here.

He missed the wind and the rain of San Francisco, and the boozy camaraderie that typified its journalism. The Times was bigger, slower, colder. The kind of flaming rewrite he had become accustomed to up north was non-existent down here.

Priorities were shifting. Times were changing.

We talked about it in a quiet moment, this time at a bar called the Redwood, when it was late and there was no one left but us, and nothing to offer but truth.

He wanted to go home again and I talked him out of it, because this was the top, this was why we had written all those words a lifetime ago, to be here, where the muscle and the money were.

Belch was never convinced, but he began dealing with misery in his own way. He quit drinking and quit smoking and started seeing a shrink. It helped at first, but then his emotional problems deepened and after awhile he was taking mood-lifting drugs.

We talked about that too, and he told me once they'd given him the wrong prescription and he began hallucinating that he was seeing Ed McMahon in his living room.

It saddened him, I think, not so much that he hallucinated, but *Ed McMahon?* He would have preferred Ella Fitzgerald. Belcher loved jazz.

Later, McMahon led a St. Patrick's Day parade in Beverly Hills and I messaged Belch that I had finally seen him in person too. Jer flashed back a memo, "Are you *sure?*"

When they told Belcher he was dying I took him to the Wellness Community in Santa Monica, where cancer patients draw on each other for the strength and style to face the uncertainties ahead, and I think it helped him.

I was with him often in the two months that followed. We talked about the people we'd known and the stories we'd written and the deadlines we'd beaten. We talked about the weather in San Francisco, and he looked at me and said quietly, "I wish it would rain."

On the day he died, his wife said, "I never saw anyone fight so hard to live. He said to me when he found out about the cancer, 'I don't want to die a wimp.' By God, Al, he was never a wimp."

I'll miss Belcher more than I have ever missed anyone, but the truths we discovered together are still stronger than tears. I'll just say goodby, Jer.

And save me a place at the bar.

— 30 —

There Ought To Be Clowns

"The mouth means
happiness all right,
but the tear lines are
personal. They're
for the family I lost
at Auschwitz."

I was talking with Jan Natarno one day and he was saying that the era of the clown, the *real* clown, is past in America.

"Being a clown used to be special," he said, looking at a photograph of himself in full makeup, "but now . . ."

He ended the sentence with a shrug and stared for awhile at the picture of the guy with the happy mouth and the tear-lined eyes and the fake diamond at the end of his nose.

Then he said, "The circus has gotten too big and a clown is just a fill-in act, something to eat up time while the props are being changed.

"Maybe," he said, "just maybe *everything* has gotten too big."

We were standing in a hallway of his Hollywood apartment where he now edits video tape for actors to send in to casting directors.

Natarno is an amiable, rubber-faced man of 56 with hair that is thinning in front and long in back. Barely five-feet two-inches tall with granny glasses hanging around his neck on a silver chain, he looks a little like one of the Seven Dwarfs.

The corridor wall was lined with photographs that showed him in three different clown modes: as Catalina Cappy, as the first Ronald McDonald and as Goo-Goo on stage at Hollywood's old Moulin Rouge.

There were also pictures of him with people like Ronald Reagan when he was governor of California, and Joe DiMaggio and Jack Benny.

I mentioned to Natarno that he looked as though he had really enjoyed being a clown and he said he had loved it, and then began talking about how the art of being a clown belonged to a past era of circus tents, before the corporations took over.

"I'll never be a clown again," he said. "The thrill is gone, and once the thrill is gone, the clown is gone."

Giving it all up after 30 years was not an easy decision for him. He was a third-generation clown, following in the footsteps of his father and his grandfather in their native Poland.

"They were the best," Natarno said. "That diamond I glued at the end of my nose is to show we played for royalty once. Kids used to ask how I made it stick and I'd say I had a hole drilled in the end of my nose and the diamond just screwed in."

I asked him if the rest of the clown makeup had any special meaning.

"Well," he said, "the three-leaf clover on my face represents one leaf for each generation of the family to perform as a clown."

"How about the rest of it?"

I wasn't really prying, I just wondered if the combination of a mouth painted into a perpetual smile and eyes with tear lines through them represented the proximity of laughter and tears.

"I suppose they do generally," Natarno said. "The mouth means happinesss all right, but the tear lines are personal. They're for the family I lost at Auschwitz."

I hadn't expected that.

The little clown with the painted smile had lost his mother, father and two younger brothers to the Nazi gas chambers and had himself survived only because he had slipped away from a holding camp and had escaped through neutral countries.

The greasepaint masked a sorrow greater than anyone could imagine.

"God," I said, "I don't know how anyone could even *start* being a clown after living through something like that."

"You do it," he said, "because you have to. Being a clown helps."

Concentrating on making someone else laugh lessened the impact of his own sorrow. The crying stopped when Cappy began cartwheeling across the stage.

For more than three decades after the war, Natarno played fairs and schools and nightclubs and even ships, sometimes working in four or five shows a day.

"You were really something when you were a clown then," he said, "but it's a different feeling today, at least in this country. Clowns are still popular in Europe, but not America. We're outmoded, gone, done with."

I have a special feeling for clowns. My mother, who hated sadness, felt that laughter was the only adequate response to childhood disaster.

I remember falling out of a tree when I was about seven. I gashed my head and knocked the wind out of myself. I was bleeding and breathless at the same time.

Mom rushed up and said, "Quick, think of something funny!"

Given short notice, I had no time to recall the humorous moments from a Laurel and Hardy movie or a Krazy Kat cartoon. The best I could come up with was a clown I had seen about a year before, so I concentrated on him.

Sure enough, my breath returned and the bleeding stopped. It was a miracle. Even today I associate the imagery of a clown with the resumption of life.

I never saw Jan Natarno perform, and I'm still sorry he gave up being a clown. Having known pain, he was probably better able to lessen it in others. The best funnymen are the saddest.

A friend of mine, in observing the non-changing nature of human conduct, used to say, "Same old circus, different clowns," but that isn't true.

The very elements that drove Natarno from the center ring make this an especially scary age. Life is becoming too complex, the circus too big. It's time to think of something funny again.

Bring back the clowns.

— 30 —

A
Lion
In The
Streets

A man alone,
with nothing but
his willingness
to die for others,
ought not to go unsung.

The small condo still smelled faintly of fire and water. Scorched wires dangled from the ceiling, and the partly melted door of a refrigerator hung open.

What had been carpeting was reduced to charred fuzz. What had been walls were blackened slabs of sheet rock.

Rafter beams lay across the bare ceiling like the cremated ribs of a dead man. A blue tarp that covered the burned-out roof cast the room in a pale, surrealistic glow.

Wind whispered through heat-blasted windows. Rain fell.

"This is where the little girl was," Mike Knieriem said, pausing in the doorway of a charred bedroom.

He stood looking for a moment, remembering, then moved down the hall to another room.

"This is where I found the little boy. It was so black in here I couldn't see. The heat was killing me. I was ready to get out. Then there was a flash of light and I saw the kid on the floor.

"I always wondered where the light came from. It was like a strobe. First I thought it was the drapes exploding, but then I realized they'd gone long ago."

He shook his head. "You've got to wonder about that."

Heroes emerge from unlikely places. In war, they're the shyest guy in the company. In peace, the quietest man on the block.

Knieriem, 46, is the quiet man, the unlikely hero. At 5-foot-6 and 130 pounds, he doesn't even *look* heroic.

He says he's just an out-of-work driver of a delivery truck, living with a wife and two sons in an ordinary suburban neighborhood and, you say, "Sure, that's Mike, that's him."

Not a lion in the street, but another guy scratching for survival, looking for a job, worrying about tomorrow.

But then . . .

Friday, Oct. 2, 10:15 p.m. Newbury Park, Ventura County.

Mike and Jan Knieriem had just returned home from watching their eldest son play football.

Jan was on the phone. Mike, getting ready for bed, had stripped to his sweat pants. No shirt, no shoes. Through an open window, he heard a cry for help.

He looked out and couldn't believe what he saw.

"There were flames shooting from the windows of a condo across the street. I knew there were two kids in there. I hollered for Jan to call 911. Then I ran."

Standing on the front porch of the burning unit was the young baby sitter of the two children who lived there: a boy, 4, a girl, 6. The baby sitter said the kids were still inside.

Knieriem didn't hesitate. The door and the doorway were sheets of flame. He took two steps into the burning building and a blast of heat knocked him to his knees.

He couldn't see. He couldn't breathe. Darkness was intensified by thick, black smoke that burned his eyes and clogged his throat.

Fire burned in glowing reds and yellows, like torches in a cave.

Mike began crawling down a hallway. The floor plan of the condo was the same as his...but in reverse. He bumped into burning walls and white-hot furniture, but he kept going.

"I opened the first bedroom door and the little girl was standing in the middle of the room crying," he said. "I grabbed her and pulled her to the front porch.

"I thought about running home and getting a wet blanket to protect myself, but I knew the boy was still in there, and, if he was going to live, I had to take my chances."

At such moments are heroes born: when instinct abates and a conscious decision prevails to risk everything for another human being.

Knieriem went back into the flames.

He groped down the hall to a second bedroom like a man crawling through hell, the entire condo now embraced in fire, temperatures soaring to 2,000 degrees.

Then that flash of light in the darkness, a small, seemingly life-less body face down on the floor. Mike grabbed him and headed out, stumbling and gasping.

The boy wasn't breathing.

"I knew nothing about oral resuscitation," Knieriem said. "But I knew I had to blow in his mouth or he was gone. I kept hollering, 'Breathe!' and pretty soon his stomach began to rise and fall . . ."

He remembers pieces of the boy's charred skin on his hands and around his mouth. Then he passed out.

The little girl recovered. Her brother is still being treated. The parents thanked Knieriem, but nothing more.

This is what happens to heroes. He was kept two days in an intensive care unit, miraculously unburned but felled by the acrid smoke. He suffered fainting spells and had difficulty breathing.

Hospital bills have amounted to $6,000. He's still out of a job and his wife works only 20 hours a week. There's no medical insurance.

Had all of that been of abiding concern to Mike Knieriem on the chilly October night he heard a cry for help, two children would surely be dead. But it wasn't, and they owe him their lives.

In a society that honors men at arms, a man alone and with nothing but his willingness to die for others ought not to go unsung.

For that searing moment in Newbury Park, a true act of heroism occurred. And a lion was in the streets.

— 30 —

A
Face
In
The
Darkness

"Just recently
I asked a doctor
to put me to sleep."

The light in Mark Basham's apartment was dim, the flattened rays of an afternoon sun filtered through louvered shades. Even so, it was not difficult to see the scars left on his face from a fire that almost killed him a dozen years ago, or the fingerless hands he tried unconsciously to keep out of sight.

Neither the pale light nor the skin grafts of a hundred operations could conceal the terrible things flames had done to him as a child in the small Kentucky town where he was born.

"Being burned," he said in hushed, almost whispery tones, "is like suddenly losing your identity. One moment your face is there, the next moment it's gone."

Photographs of the face that no longer exists, the Mark Basham that disappeared in a flash of heat, hung on two nearby walls, to remind him of the features that had once been his. The photographs stamped the room with a dreadful reality.

Mark sat tucked in a corner of the couch that was one of the few pieces of furniture in the apartment, as though by sitting in shadow he was seeking even deeper anonymity in an already lightless environment.

We talked about the face that the fire had left him.

"The doctor wouldn't let me look in a mirror when they took the bandages off," he said. "But I saw myself reflected in the plastic above my bed, and I cried. It didn't seem real."

He was 12 when it happened. Mark's stepfather was using gasoline to remove glue from the floor of a house they had just rented. The glue had been used to hold carpeting down. The stepfather left the room to light a cigarette. There was an explosion . . . .

"I remember trying to climb out a window over a clothes dryer. The dryer was hot and I fell off. It was like I was moving in slow motion. When I finally got out, everything speeded up. I was burned black. There was no pain then. Just heat, then chills. The pain came later."

16

Mark was burned over most of his body. His mother and brother died in the fire. His stepfather disappeared. He hasn't seen him since.

Today, Mark is a tall, slim 24. His face scars are muted but apparent. Only thumbs remain on each hand.

He telephoned me first not to talk specifically about the fire but to tell me about a bus driver who had ordered him off a bus because he didn't want to look at Mark.

We discussed briefly what he called "my disfigurement," and the pain the disfigurement was causing him in a society that places high priority on appearance.

"The bus driver wanted me where he couldn't see me," Mark told me at the time. "He wanted me out of the way. He said when he saw me at a bus stop, he wasn't going to stop."

I offered to go to Mark's home and talk with him about it. He declined. He wanted a telephone interview. He didn't want me to see him. I asked him to think about it, and he said he would.

That was a year ago. I didn't hear from him again until last week. This time a doughnut shop had fired him "because of the way I look." He invited me to his apartment.

"I don't go around with a chip on my shoulder," he said, when I suggested that might be his problem. "People don't like to look at me. That's a fact and it hurts."

"Sometimes teen-agers will drive by and holler 'Hey, Freddie!' He was the monster in the movie 'Nightmare on Elm Street.' Another bus driver thought I had AIDs and didn't want me to breathe on him. People will sometimes just stop and stare."

He has difficulty finding work because of the way he looks. He lives on Social Security checks. His housing is subsidized. Sometimes during the day he visits a nearby center for homeless people with mental problems. He feels comfortable with them.

Mark vacillates between hope for the future and utter despair. He denies nightmares, then discusses them. He claims not to recall much of the fire, then describes it in vivid detail.

"I haven't had a fair shake in life. I want to be around others to let them know that people like me exist. I want a job that will take me out in the open."

But then he thinks about the 100 skin grafts and the 20 sessions of reconstructive surgery he has undergone and all the surgery that lies ahead.

"Looking back, I would have rather died than to go through all that. I don't want to go through it again. Just recently I asked a doctor to put me to sleep. I can't take the pain anymore . . . ."

We talked into the early evening, until the light inside the apartment had grown even dimmer and the photographs of the other Mark merged into the shadows. I asked what I could do for him, and he said, "Help me find work." I promised to try.

As he walked me to the door, we stopped to look closely at one of his pre-fire pictures. Mark stared at it for a long time and finally said there was one thing about the fire that he could be grateful for. It had left him only stubs for ears.

He looked at me straight-on for the first time and said, "I never did like my ears."

I didn't know whether to laugh or cry.

— 30 —

A Quiet Moment With Joe

We look at so much,
but see so little. The
Joes of the world fade
into the background
of emerging issues.
They rarely lead
a parade.

Joe Sammaritano stepped with authority into the face of the traffic and held at full arm's length a red and white sign that said *Stop*. He is a slight man, barely 5 feet 4 inches tall, but there was dignity in his manner, and the moving cars on Serrania Avenue obligingly halted at the crosswalk.

Then, and only then, did Joe smile and motion a group of waiting children across the street. One of them hugged him and said, "Thanks, grandpa."

He's there every morning, noon and afternoon, the old guy in front of Serrania Avenue Elementary School, shepherding the kids from one side of the busy street to the other. Joe the crossing guard.

"You don't fool around on this job," he explained one sweet morning, on a day before the heat came. Children gathered around him as he stood under a pepper tree, ever alert for little ones who wanted to get across the street.

"You don't know who's driving these days. Drunks, dopers. They might kill the kids if I wasn't there. One car ran right on through just yesterday and I hit the window with the sign. That didn't stop him. He just kept going. Look what it did to the sign."

He held up the stop sign to show a slight chip, glaring in remembered anger. "That made me madder than hell. But then, a woman who went through came by the next day and apologized. She hadn't been paying attention. I told her to be careful."

Joe is 73 years old, a retired garment presser with a slight Italian accent. He earns $6 an hour as a crossing guard, which helps pay the bills for him and for Lilly, his wife of 47 years. He has been helping kids cross the street since 1978.

I knew Joe before I ever spoke to him. The Woodland Hills school lies along my path through the Valley. I had noticed him because of the way the children responded to him. They seemed always clustered around Joe. Some called him grandpa, others pop. More than one hugged him.

20

I decided then I wanted to write about Joe. But life is a series of challenges with little time left for quiet moments, and many months have passed since the first time I saw him. We look at so much, but see so little. The Joes of the world fade into the background of emerging issues. They rarely lead a parade.

But there was a reason other than that and even other than the man himself that finally compelled me to stop and talk to Joe.

I have a good feeling about Serrania.

Years ago, on the first day of school busing in Los Angeles, I was assigned to visit elementary schools to see how kids bused from the inner city were greeted by their peers. What I observed at Serrania was not so much the kids as the teachers.

One especially caught my eye. I don't remember her name, but I remember she knelt to one knee and helped a little boy from the ghetto remove his coat. Then she held his face gently in both hands and said, "We're so glad you're here."

I knew she meant it by the way she said it, and even though busing went down the tube three years later, the memory of that moment remains for me and, I hope, for the kid from the ghetto.

The story, by the way, never ran. Quiet times don't always make it when big events are clanging in the city.

"These are good kids," Joe was saying. The school bell had rung and he was off duty for the morning. "You can't help but like 'em. They trust me. Up until about 10, you know, they're still innocent. Sometimes they bring me their problems. A boy needed 20 cents to call home. I lent it to him. He paid me back the next day."

The school had a fund-raising drive. The children sold candy for $1 a bar. Joe ended up buying nine bars because he couldn't say no to the little people who gathered around him. He doesn't eat candy.

Albert Gross came down the street slowly, using a cane, a dapper little man about Joe's size in a snap-brim Panama hat.

"He'll be 93 soon," Joe said, watching him approach. He passes this way twice a day. We talk about the weather. *Today it's going to rain, today is going to be a good day . . . .*"

"A beautiful day," Albert said, stopping.

"Perfect," Joe replied.

"It's a mile and a quarter around the block," Albert said. "I put in 2 1/2 miles every day. I live with my daughter. She says it's good for me." He laughed as though he might not believe that.

"Albert is going to live forever," Joe said gently.

"Pretty soon I'll be blind," Albert said. "There's nothing they can do about it. I went to San Francisco and they examined me for three hours. It's hopeless. I'll have to remember things when I'm blind. I won't be able to see anymore."

I stood with Joe a very long time. I watched the children come to school and I watched Albert Gross walk slowly down the block, the young beginning to see, the old trying to remember.

I watched Joe smile at the children in a manner that was especially gentle and I watched him stand face to the traffic, sign held high, 5 feet 4 inches of human dignity, of protection, of caring.

It was not a very significant moment. But I will remember it a long, long time.

— 30 —

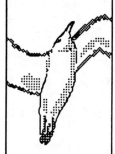

Seeing
The
Ocean
Again

I had never seen
so much emotion in
anyone over 9. We
are accustomed to
cool out here. Cool
at any cost.

I was attracted to the man by the intensity of his stare. He was standing on the beach at Venice on an early morning, the wind in his face and the waves at his feet, transfixed by something he apparently was seeing beyond the breakers, oblivious to the water that soaked his shoes.

His hair was beginning to thin and he was wearing clothes that seemed as old and rumpled as he was. They hung like rags on a scarecrow.

As I approached, he glanced over at me, turned back to the ocean and said, "Will you look at that?"

I followed his stare but saw only a Pacific turned silver by the coming day.

"Will I look at what?"

I kept thinking he might have spotted Morgan Fairchild swimming naked near the breakwater.

"The ocean!" he said with enthusiasm that seemed about to explode.

Another nut flying on mescaline.

"I've seen it before," I said with a sigh, and began to move on.

"You're lucky," the man said. He turned to me full-face and added with pride of accomplishment, "This is my first time."

His name was Hank Ketlin and he had arrived at the ocean that very morning after driving in from a place called Thayer, Kan. He had never seen the ocean before.

"Have you ever actually *been* on the ocean?" Hank asked after introductions.

"Well, yes," I said, "many times."

"In a boat?"

"In a boat."

"Hoo," he said, "that must have been something."

He stomped his feet in the surf a couple of times, splashing water like shards of crystal into the diagonals of sunlight that sliced over the rooftops.

24

I couldn't believe the man. He was like a kid at a birthday party. I had never seen so much emotion in anyone over 9. We are accustomed to cool out here. Cool at any cost.

"I can't believe that horizon," Hank said.

I looked at the horizon. It was one I had seen thousands of times. I tried to imagine it was my first view, but that never works. Wonder is a passing magic, glimpsed once and gone forever.

But still, it was a magnificent horizon at that, wide and sweeping in its scope, tantalizing in its unknowns.

"All my life," Hank said, "I've wanted to see the ocean. Dad was in the Navy during the war and gave me one of those large sea shells he'd brought back from Dago."

Dago? San Diego? Do they still call it Dago? They do in Thayer, Kan., I guess.

"He used to tell me to hold it up to my ear and I could hear the ocean winds blow." He thought about it for a while and then said, "I think it was ceramic but I still heard the wind."

There just didn't seem good enough reason and there was never enough money to come to the ocean before, Hank told me. But Mary had died two weeks ago and there were no children so there didn't seem good enough reason not to come anymore. Hank was alone now.

He had just packed up and headed west in his 1972 Chevrolet Nova, pulling a U-Haul trailer and still hearing the ocean winds. He just wished Mary could have been there with him.

"Lookit there!" he said so suddenly I thought he'd spotted a Russian sub. It was a sailboat tacking into the wind, its clean bow slicing through the flying spray.

As we stared, the boat keeled to port, its multicolored mainsail (shades of orange and magenta) sweeping over the wave tips, then spiking upright, teeth to the wind, heading for open water.

"Jesus!" Hank said. He realized what he had said and apologized. "I don't usually talk that way."

"That's all right," I said. "You may be the first person I've ever known who doesn't talk that way."

Hank had seen the ocean on television and in the movies, of course. They showed fairly current movies in Thayer. But this was the real thing. Sea air you could smell and water you could touch. I didn't tell him the sea was toxic and the fish were dying. We didn't talk about the smog that sits along the horizon when the Santa Anas blow.

They weren't important now. A man was seeing the ocean for

the very first time, an ocean of expanse and strength and life-giving vitality; an ocean of patience and beauty and dark currents of mystery.

The wonder deserved respect.

But time and magic are fleeting transitions and Hank had to leave. He was on his way to Long Beach to catch a ferry for Santa Catalina Island. "It isn't really being on the ocean," he apologized, "but it's close."

He pulled himself reluctantly away from the edge of the surf, torn between what he owned at that sunrise moment and what he was about to experience. We shook hands. He took one last look at the sea and then strode quickly toward his car.

"Hank!" I called after him.

He turned. I wanted to say something, but I didn't know what. I liked the man. And I liked seeing the ocean, the brand new ocean, through his eyes.

"I'm sorry about Mary," I said.

I'm not sure he heard me. He waved and was gone.

I stood there for a long time, a native Californian, seeing the Pacific for the very first time, and grateful beyond words to a man named Hank.

— 30—

Bad Luck Bob and His Dog

Dog owners were
battling with children
owners over the question
of who ought to be
leashed, the dogs
or the kids . . . .

Bob Greene is the kind of guy who, if there were one hole in the ground within a 10,000-mile radius, would fall into it and break his leg. Then, when he got out of the hole and sued the hole owner, he would lose the case and be successfully countersued for falling into an unauthorized hole.

Later he would suffer a deadly deep-hole virus that would cause his hair, his teeth and his fingernails to fall out. He would lose his home and his life savings to medical bills and legal costs, his wife would run off with the hole owner and his carnivorous plant would try to eat him.

Believe me when I tell you that misfortune sticks to the man like drool to a baby.

For those who may not recall Robert Alan Greene, he was arrested last March in Laurel Canyon Park for walking his dog.

Forget that the park was probably the worst place on earth to be at the time. Dog owners were battling with children owners over the question of who ought to be leashed, the dogs or the kids, and Animal Regulation Cops were swarming over the hills like Jewish commandos at an Arab outpost.

Dogcatchers, as a police friend pointed out, are usually people who cannot qualify to be *real* policemen and take out their career frustrations on whoever happens to be in the vicinity during periods of high tension.

Bob Greene, of course, was the one strolling by.

The way Bob tells it, his dog Princess was on a leash. The way the animal cops tell it, Princess was walking next to him *unleashed* and was snarling and looking around for babies to kill.

An officer shouted for Greene to stop, but Bob said he had witnessed the "Gestapo tactics" of the animal cops before and was not about to submit to their torture and humiliation and gruesome death. So he told them that and kept going.

Bad news. Bob fell into the hole again.

"I probably shouldn't have said that," he reflected during a more reasonable moment the other day. "I have a big mouth."

28

The animal cops thought so, too. Greene says they waited in the bushes, jumped him, beat him and booked both him and the dog. The dog was later o.r.'d, but Greene was charged with resisting arrest and failing to keep his pet on a leash.

He requested a jury trial, acted as his own attorney and, of course, lost.

"I was a fool," Bob lamented.

Somewhere along the way, incidentally, he had mortgaged his house in Laurel Canyon to buy a sign-making business. The business naturally failed and he lost the house.

But wait. We're not finished.

Bob was arrested that first time on March 31. He remembers it because it was Palm Sunday, but that didn't do him any good at all. And it didn't improve his luck or his judgment. Four months later, he went back to the park and this time, he admits, was walking Princess *without* a leash.

"Bob," I asked him as gently as I could, "why in the dog-walking hell did you go *back* to Laurel Canyon after that first incident and not even put the dog on a leash this time?"

He thought about that for a moment, then shook his head sadly.

"I don't know," he said. "I guess it was just bad timing on my part."

Greene is 55 and, as one might expect, divorced. We met in the West Hollywood sign-making shop he once owned and now works for. He sleeps in a tiny room adjacent to the office. Princess and a stray called Barney sleep in the room with him when they are not out hunting babies.

"I'd do some things all over again now if I could," he said. I hope to God he would.

Sparing you the strange details of that second encounter at Laurel Canyon Park, Bob was subsequently charged with abandoning a pet, interfering with a dog officer and threatening a dog officer.

He is to appear in Municipal Court on those charges unless he is already in jail after sentencing on the first set of convictions.

"When I was found guilty," Greene remembered, "the judge gave me a choice of being sentenced right away or of waiting until October. I asked him what he would suggest and he said, 'Well, if I sentence you now, you'll go straight to jail.' So I said I'd wait until October."

Greene and others involved in the Laurel Canyon Park mess insist that he is being punished not for crimes he committed but for twice testifying before the Animal Regulation Commission on the excesses of the dog cops.

Maybe so, but if bad judgment were a felony, Bob Greene might be sitting on Death Row today.

As a final example of his synaptic lapses, I asked if he were going to appeal the first conviction.

"I sure am," he said. "A friend of mine is going to show me how to fill out the papers. I'm doing it myself."

Oh my goodness, oh my soul, there goes Robert down the hole.

Again.

ALL
OUR
SONS

"Dying is healing too, you know."

There's something special about the boy, a joy so bountiful and a life so resilient that to depict him now as a sackful of shredded dreams would be to ignore the abundance of light he has brought to the darkness that surrounds him.

In his 16 years, some of it painful beyond words, Jason Simon has maintained a balance that few achieve, much less sustain, through judgments of the soul that reduce us at the end to whimpers. Dying is not the best thing we do.

I write of him today not because easy words lie in a young man's fight with cancer, but because the boy elevates the human spirit to a degree one rarely observes.

When I first met Jason, he was hunched forward in his bed, coughing violently and trying to breathe. A slim tube of oxygen ran from a tank to his nose, and another carried morphine into a vein of his arm. A humidifier hissed steam into the heavy air.

I am uneasy with the pain of others, especially the young, and tend to retreat in haste from scenes of anguish. I did so in this case by asking Jason's parents to let him rest and to tell me about him in the living room downstairs.

Jason learned of his illness by accident when, at 13, he fell and hurt his leg. X-rays revealed not the consequences of the fall, but a rare form of cancer. The doctor was frank: The boy could lose his leg, even his life.

The shock was stunning. This was youth in the apex of innocence called upon to consider its own demise. Jason said nothing to the doctor, but later turned to his step-mother. "Mom," he said with a sweetness that claws at the heart, "I could die."

This is a family of "born-again" Christians. How much that had to do with Jason's strength during the next three years might never be determined, but, quite obviously, it counted.

After six operations, two years of chemotherapy and more pain than most of us could ever imagine, Jason was asked by his father if he still had faith.

32

He replied by holding up a thumb and a forefinger to indicate an infinitesimal distance and said: "I'm this close to God. Why would I blow it now?"

Seated across from each other downstairs, the parents drew a loving portrait of a son who ran through the summers of his youth with innocent abandon, never dreaming to what dark end the race would take him.

"A loving, tender, caring boy," Donna Simon called him.

"A boy who has never given up," his father said.

I heard this also from teachers at Monroe High, where, up until two months ago, Jason had been a student.

"I have not seen such a joy of life in anyone in 25 years of teaching," one of them said.

From others:

"He wanted no special treatment. He wanted to earn everything he got. He never wanted to be considered a dying kid."

"He cares more for others than for himself. He stays strong for the sake of us."

Even as the disease spread, Jason drew from living what he could, but the quest was more altruistic than selfish.

"He never wanted to make anyone feel bad," a student said. "He kept all the hurting for himself."

He touched his classmates so deeply that they have begun on their own to raise funds for a scholarship in their friend's honor.

How much pain Jason was enduring became clear in September when he announced that he wanted no more chemotherapy. Told he could be dead within six months, he said softly, "I've done all I can."

The coughing from upstairs stopped. I asked the Simons if I could see Jason again. They led me once more to his room.

He was sitting up in bed this time, smiling. His eyes were as bright as spring. No fever glowed there. I spoke inanities, but even they took on significance with Jason's replies.

"You look good," I said, which was true.

"The problem isn't on the outside," Jason said. "It's on the inside."

I asked how he felt.

"I could never explain it," he replied. "How do you describe the color red to a blind man?"

Then he said, "I've done the best I could for myself and my family, but now I'm tired and I want something to happen."

Asked what he thought would happen, he said, "I'm trusting

God to heal me either way." Pause. "Dying is healing too, you know."

Dylan Thomas understood the relationship between life and nature when he wrote: *The force that through the green fuse drives the flowers drives my green age; that blasts the roots of trees is my destroyer.*

There is inevitability to the patterns that surround us and, like trees, we fall someday. Still, I'm angered by the darkness that claims one so young.

"Even when you trust in the Lord," Donna Simon said, "a little boy is still scared."

I left the house on Septo Street less saddened than overwhelmed by a sense of joy more prominent than pain.

I thought of Dylan Thomas then, too, and of those immense forces that claim the young too soon:

And I am dumb to tell the crooked rose my youth is bent by the same wintry fever . . . .

(Editor's note: Jason Simon died last night.)

— 30 —

Kris
and
John

"Mark who?

The older man looks a little like John Houseman, with his droll manner and his arched eyebrows, and the younger guy like maybe Kris Kristofferson in one of his scragglier modes.

They are sitting side by side at a crowded bar when I wander in to escape the bitter weather.

Well, maybe not bitter, but it *seemed* bitter if you get my meaning. A little mist on the Valley.

I was supposed to meet my wife at 7 o'clock in front of the place but I was there at 6:30, because I am always early, no matter where I go.

So I decide that a little something to fight the dampness would be good. I drift inside and find the only stool at the bar and order some Glenlivet on the rocks with just a dash of water.

And I begin listening to John and Kris.

John is having a Manhattan and is holding the glass with the tips of his fingers. Kris is drinking Corona beer from the bottle, and sometimes it drools down onto his matted beard. He is making no effort to wipe it away.

The slobbery is driving John crazy and he keeps throwing admonishing glances toward Kris, who seems not to notice.

Kris wears a kind of faint smile and just keeps staring straight ahead at the bottles that line the shelves in back of the bar.

Finally, John can take it no longer, and you know what he says? He looks right at Kris and says in a kind of slurred and cultured voice, "Have you ever heard of Samuel Clemens?"

That's what caught my attention.

Kris turns to face him directly and says, "What?"

"I asked you, sir, if you had ever heard of Samuel Clemens?"

Most of us would probably just say no and turn away, but Kris seems delighted that someone is talking to him.

"No," he says, "is he from around here?"

This is exactly what John wants.

"Samuel Clemens," John says, sitting up in a kind of arrogant attitude, "was Mark Twain!"

Kris says, "Mark who?"

I don't think John expected that.

"You don't know who Mark Twain is?" he says, genuinely surprised.

Kris shrugs and says, "You want another one of those pink drinks? On me."

"Thank you," John says, "I would like another, yes."

So the cowboy orders two more and says, "Who's the guy you're talking about?"

John, who is momentarily disarmed by Kris' generosity, softens the sting in his voice and says, "Probably the most famous writer in American history."

Kris seems interested.

"Oh yeah? What'd he write?"

"What did he *write?*" John says in the midst of a coughing fit. "I can't believe this! I have never spoken to anyone in all my 68 years who did not know what Mark Twain wrote!"

Kris smiles. "Oh yeah?"

"That pleases you?" John says, incredulously.

Kris shrugs. The simple gesture seems to infuriate John in a kind of patrician way, and I am sitting there thinking that it would probably be the first bar fight I have ever seen based on literature.

I have seen fights over broads, cars and football teams, and even over whether Jesus could have made it as a general contractor, but never over authors.

The closest I saw to that, I guess, was an argument that developed over the comparative intellectual merits of Tawny Little and Kelly Lange, who, for those ignorant of media stars, specialize in Southern California's cotton candy news.

Kelly learned TV journalism as a weather girl and Tawny as a beauty queen, which gives you a pretty good idea how limited the intellectual debate might be.

Back at the bar, John can hardly contain himself.

"Tell me, sir," he says, "what country are you from?"

He means it in pure sarcasm, of course, but Kris takes it as a legitimate question and says cheerfully, "From America. The accent is Oregonian."

John looks at him and kind of shakes his head like he can't quite believe this is all happening.

"Oregonians don't have accents," he says.

John finishes his drink and is about to leave when he realizes he owes Kris a drink.

"Would you like another one of those?" he says with uncon-
cealed distaste.

"Why, you bet yer Bo Diddley I would," Kris says in his Oregonian accent.

While the bartender is bringing them the drink, Kris says suddenly, "You know when Poe died?"

John looks at him for a long time and says, "Poe?"

"Yeah," Kris says, "the guy who wrote . . ."

"I *know* what he wrote!" John says, annoyed.

"But," Kris says, holding up one finger, "do you know when
he died?"

"This is preposterous," John says, standing.

"You don't know," Kris says in a kind of teasing tone.

"If I knew," John says, thick brows lowered over piercing
eyes, "I would not share it with you!"

He heads for the door without even finishing his drink, but before he can get out, Kris shouts, "1849!"

Then he reaches over and drinks the rest of John's Manhattan.
I was pleased to see that he left the maraschino cherry.

— 30 —

FAMILY

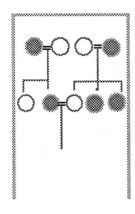

For
the Love
of
Shana Lee

One flower lives . . . .

I keep seeing the face of the boy, a child of 3, looking out at the world through troubled eyes. His expression is pensive, a look caught in the microsecond of reflection, a thought emulsified on film, trapped and frozen, the fading spirit of a young life ended.

Who killed Joey Phelps?

The question haunts me.

Who caused him pain? Who triggered soft whimpers in the night? Who finally and with savage brutality struck the blow that damped the last tiny ember of his life?

Who is responsible and why did they do it?

A picture appeared in Friday's editions. Joey Phelps was beaten to death in the bedroom of his home. His injuries, a coroner's assistant said, were like "being hit by a truck."

Joey's mother and her boyfriend are accused of felony child abuse. The mother is also charged with manslaughter.

On the night of Joey's death, a neighbor heard heavy thumping that went on for an hour in the moments past midnight.

Then she heard a soft whimper.

And then there was silence.

In that silence, the heart of Joey Phelps stopped beating, an almost imperceptible disruption in the rhythms of life that pulse around us.

In that instant, he became a face in a photo, a snippet of news that will fade with the passing days.

But Joey left a special imprint on my life, and I'll tell you why.

I'm no stranger to death. I have walked through dark shadows for many years as a Marine at war and a journalist at work.

I have heard cries of pain in such awful vibrato that decades later they enribbon my sleep.

But still . . . .

I see Joey's face with all of its bright promise and sad vision and it troubles me. Given the circumstances of his fate, it would trouble me at any time, but especially it bothers me today, for there is a sudden sweetness in my own life.

I have a new friend.

Her name is Shana Lee and she was born to the world on a gleaming, wind-swept morning into a family that adores her.

She's beautiful and I'm crazy about her.

"I keep doing this," her pixie mother said to me, "just so you'll have something more to write about."

Then she handed me that special little girl and said, "Meet Shana Lee."

I held her in my arms and shared the life burning within her, as elemental as the howling night winds that brushed pastels into the dawn of her birth.

I heard small sounds from new lips and touched the tips of fingers that would one day reach for stars.

"Shana Lee," I said to her mother, "is one hell of a baby."

I held her for a long time, quieting the cries, rocking her gently into sleep, leaving her tucked in soft blankets in a room warm with love.

I returned from the hospital still filled with the wonder of my new friend. . .and was confronted by the picture of Joey Phelps.

A colleague had left it on my desk because, I'm sure, he felt the same pain I would feel when I looked at the little boy's face and tried to imagine the reach of his anguish in the last terrible seconds of life.

An existence so new, so violently ended.

The picture was left for me to absorb and write about by someone who could never anticipate the dichotomy of emotions it would produce on this special day, or the tones of irony that would shape this column.

I find in the death of Joey a message of brutality that fills me with great sadness, as I find in the birth of Shana Lee a message of love that fills me with elation.

Here was a boy of significant promise brought into a world of troubled circumstances, gone without a chance to ever reach up and out, to touch the stars that Shana Lee will touch.

Who knows what Joey Phelps could have given the world?

Who knows what bright potential gleamed in eyes so suddenly robbed of light?

Life deals us futures laced with chance. Some survive the capricious odds, some don't. One flower lives, another dies. Both share the same sun, the same earth, the same rain.

What genetic acids blend to destroy a Joey Phelps and what wonders combine to give us Shana Lee? What blesses one and condemns the other?

That isn't a new question and there isn't a good answer, but I'll keep asking it and so will you, until someplace down the road we can isolate the factors of savagery that conspire to take a little boy's life on a dark and lonely night.

I hadn't intended this as a Requiem for Joey Phelps, because the wonder of Shana Lee is so much with me.

I had only meant to chronicle the sweet, funny, panicky, worrisome moments of birth and greet with trumpets the new friend who will walk with me over trails she has never walked before.

A friend through whose eyes I will view life in tones of color I had not noticed in the past.

Welcome to the world, Shana Lee. Welcome to the world, glowing beauty.

And, oh yes . . . goodby, Joey Phelps.

— 30 —

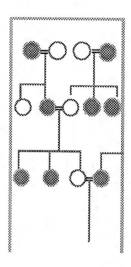

Under
the
Deck

...I doubt there's
a man alive who
can match my facility
at resisting the job
of taking out the
garbage.

The nature of man is to resist and, by resisting, to snap the shackles of slavery, to topple history's tyrants and, if possible, to do as little as possible around the house.

I'm good at that.

I'm not sure how I'd do at chain-snapping or tyrant-toppling, but I doubt there's a man alive who can match my facility at resisting the job of taking out the garbage.

I am to garbage-ducking what Joe Dimaggio was to baseball. In one memorable 1973 streak, I achieved 56 consecutive garbage-free days, a record that is still regarded with respect wherever men gather to drink beer and discuss greatness.

But champions, by the nature of their concentration, often excel in only one arena of expertise. Big Bill Tilden, I am told, couldn't dance, nor could Swingin' Sammy Snead carry a tune.

Similarly, while I am a whiz at garbage-ducking, I was unable to further avoid the stuff under the deck. I knew you'd care.

First, I hate clutter. If I lived alone, it would be in rooms without furniture. A used desk for my word processor and an orange crate to sit on, but nothing else.

Folks would peek in and say, "My, what an orderly old fellow," and I would wiggle my nose at them like Ollie North and wink and say, "Have a nice day!"

Which brings us to disorder.

We have a large wooden deck at our house. Until recently it was filled with chairs, chaise longues, tables and barbecue pits. Their random deployment offended my sense of symmetry.

I love . . . well . . . *emptiness.*

"What good is a deck with nothing on it?" my wife would ask.

I'd reply by saying simply, "God did not give us wood to cover it with tubed aluminum," which I hoped was vague enough to explain an otherwise unexplainable aversion to clutter.

It did no good. The deck remained packed with things to sit on and eat at and barbecue hamburgers with.

46

But then, not long ago, something wonderful happened. We had a wedding at our house, which required that everything on the deck be temporarily placed *under* it. And there it has been ever since, despite almost unbearable pressure to restore the deck to its original state.

Last weekend, however, came a moment of truth.

"I've reached the end of my patience, Elmer," my wife said.

She calls me that because sometimes I slur my name so that it sounds like Elmer Teenez. It's a family joke, like backing out of the driveway and running over your own dog.

"How can I possibly move that stuff back on the deck alone?" I whined.

"Hire a Mexican," she said.

"I *am* a Mexican," I said.

"Hire a *strong* Mexican who is willing to work and doesn't whine."

"If I could sing 'La Bamba,' you wouldn't be pushing me around this way."

"I can't sing 'La Bamba' either," she said, "so I'll help. You go under the deck and pass the stuff up, and I'll put it in place."

I crawled under the deck. Diagonals of sunlight slanted through the openings between the floorboards. They gave the stored furniture a surrealistic look.

"Hey," I shouted up to the deck top, "this is pretty!"

"I'm glad you're enjoying it, " my wife called down.

"It's like a Van Gogh painting."

"I don't believe Van Gogh ever did an under-the-deck scene," her voice said.

"Monet?"

"Stop stalling and pass up the furniture," the voice demanded.

I felt like I was talking to God.

I crawled in farther. The space narrowed. Cobwebs brushed my face. If there is anything I hate worse than clutter, it is spiders. Well, spiders and moths. I had an idea for a television movie once about moths.

"Remember the moth idea?" I called up.

"Was that the one with the sex slaves?"

"Sex *volunteers,"* I corrected.

"What about it?" she said impatiently.

"I was just remembering it."

"Stop with the memory lane and pass up the . . . oh, never mind."

I heard footsteps. Then she stuck her head under the deck.

"You go topside," she said, "and *I'll* hand up the furniture."

"This is a man's job," I insisted.

"I know," she said, "but it's too late to go out and get one now."

When she saw my lower lip begin to tremble, she said, "I'm just kidding."

I'm good at getting my lower lip to tremble.

"You're not kidding," I said. "You've always wished I were a cowboy."

The balance was shifting in my favor. Women cannot stand to see a man in emotional pain.

"No," she said, a little too wistfully, "not really. I'd just like someone a little more willing to help around the house."

"You should have married a handyman."

My eyes fluttered.

"Tell you what," she said quickly. "It's getting late, so we'll skip the furniture today. I'll go up and fix us a margarita in honor of your race. Would that be better?"

"Sí."

I'd done it again. Another weekend without deck-clutter. I smell a new record.

She went inside and whipped up the margaritas. I sat on a box and hummed "La Bamba."

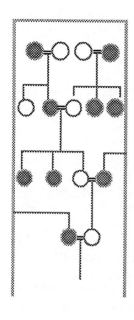

Heeding
the Winds
of Change

. . . a whisper in the wind . . . .

His name is Marty. I last saw him at the front of the house, his tan Toyota bulging with the bare essentials of a life he was about to start. At 20, he was heading out on his own, responding to a whisper of independence that was blowing in the wind, a call to see new places and hear new sounds.

I asked him how he felt as we stood together near the large oak that sheltered the driveway, where we had stood so many times before. He smiled slightly and said, "A little nervous, I guess."

"That's pretty normal," I said. "We've all gone through it. But sooner or later a kid's got to leave the nest. It's scary, but we stumble on through somehow. You'll do all right."

"I hope so. I'm going to try."

"I know you will."

We talked for a long time. I was trying to come up with the kind of advice that might do him some good as he began building an adulthood high up at the northern end of California, where the redwoods march to the edge of the sea, where a roaring surf dares the granite cliffs.

But all I could come up with were a lot of rambling basics Marty had already mastered simply by reaching 20. Drive carefully, work hard, be honest, clean your room, keep the music down, do your homework and, for God's sake, leave my clothes alone.

"Your clothes are safe," he said, laughing. "I won't be here, remember?"

So he won't.

That's going to take some getting used to. An empty boy's room with posters on the wall. No rock music rattling the windows. The vacancy. The silence.

Marty?

He had actually decided months ago that L.A. was no longer for him. It wasn't an easy decision. He was torn between the security of life at home and a whisper on the wind that said *be your own man!* That said *spread your wings, boy!* That said *fly!*

50

The voice in his head was compelling, and in the end he responded to the call that came from beyond the distance, from the shadows of the ridge line, from the sunlight in the glades.

I considered trying to talk him out of the north coast as his destination. Eureka isn't exactly a land of opportunity. The weather isn't ideal.

But I kept my silence because opportunity is what you make it to be, and because someone told me a long time ago that a man grows tall under dark skies, when the storm howls and the rain falls, and I think I know what he meant.

Mart was simply following my lead. I have always loved the open land and have talked about it for years. He must have been listening.

The north coast is honest country. Redwoods dwarf our fussy priorities, and the wild rivers rush down from the mountains with a strength that defies containment. There are lessons there for the young, far beyond what I could teach on the front porch, with only minutes left.

Still, there had to be something I could say, something vital, something important, something to strengthen him in the hard times, to cheer him in the sad times. Something real, something fine. *Something . . . .*

Not that I haven't had the opportunity to do all that before. I have known the boy for a lot of years. It's just that I never got around to it, or maybe I didn't even know what to say then, or maybe I was just too damned preoccupied with writing words and meeting deadlines and responding to the whispers in my own head.

Time is measured by different standards. We had an apple tree in the yard once and I used to promise myself that Mart and I were going to go off somewhere and talk before the apples were all gone. I'd tell him what life was all about and prepare him for the tomorrows which then seemed so distant.

But I never did, not that way, and then one day I'd realize that the last apple had fallen from the tree and it was too late. Time had passed and I hadn't even noticed.

Damn me and damn the days that fly too fast, the years that flicker by like fireflies in the night.

"Well," he said with a mixture of reluctance and anticipation, "I guess I'd better leave."

I nodded. "The traffic shouldn't be too bad," I said.
Is that what I would leave him with?
A traffic report? That's all?

We shook hands, the small hand grown large that I had once held as we walked through the summers of his youth, the hand I had touched as he slept in a crib long turned to kindling, the hand I had taken to pull him up over a hilltop where we hiked.

"So long, Dad."

"So long, Mart."

We hugged, and as we did it suddenly came to me, advice beyond planning, a word drawn from that area within us where all good instincts are born.

I said simply, "Care."

And then my son's car pulled from the driveway, and then it was a disappearing blur of tan down a long and winding road, and then it was gone. I stood there for a very long time, listening to the wind blow.

— 30 —

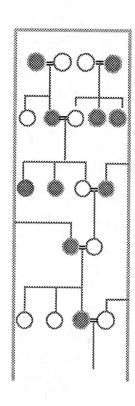

Welcome
to the
World

A small, perfect life . . . .

Our bedroom door opened at exactly 12.30 a.m. I was in a deep sleep.

"Dad," my son said, shaking me, "her water broke."

I said, "What?"

"Her water broke."

"What?"

I tend to repeat when confused.

"She's got to go to the hospital."

"Who?"

"Lisa!"

"What's wrong with her?"

"She's going to have a baby!"

I am not one of those who snaps awake in the middle of the night. I was therefore still staring and trying to figure out if I should call a plumber or a hydrologist when my wife, who wakes up running, crawled over me.

"Out of the way, Elmer," she said, "great events are occurring."

And then I remembered. We were having a baby.

My son and his wife have been staying with us for the birth. They had come down from the wild coast country of Northern California to be with experienced people. My wife handled it nicely. I stepped on the dog.

Hoover is about as dumb an animal as God ever created. He instantly plunged headlong into the closet door and bounced away barking at the ceiling.

"All right," I hollered, "everybody calm!"

"Everybody is calm," my wife said, "except you and the dog."

"You get the car warmed up," I said, "I'll call the Coast Guard."

"Maybe you'd better rest," my son said.

I've never been good at this sort of thing, but it was worst this time. I'm out of practice.

54

"When talent fails," an old city editor once told me, "rely on instinct. When instinct fails, a dry martini helps."

I headed for my mobile martini cart.

"What are you doing?" my wife asked.

"Getting ready for the baby," I said. "Where's the vermouth?"

She froze me with a look that can wither daisies.

"On second thought," I said, "I'll wait until later to celebrate."

"You're a wise man, Elmer."

I'm called Elmer because sometimes I slur my name and it sounds like Elmer Teenez.

I turned to stride away and stepped on Hoover again. He ran into the living room and began barking at the couch.

"Damn, dog," I hollered after him, "stay out from under my feet."

"Thank God it wasn't the baby," my wife said.

I pulled the car out front and waited. Five minutes passed. Ten. Fifteen. I could see myself presiding over the birth in the back seat of my company Pontiac. I'm not sure that's allowable.

"Let's go!" I shouted toward the front door.

No response.

I went inside the house. My son was calmly packing a bag. My wife was looking for the latest New Yorker magazine.

"Why the hell isn't everyone ready?" I demanded. "Where's Lisa?"

"Brushing her teeth," my son said.

"What?"

"Are we going to go through *that* again?" he asked.

"Brushing her teeth, why?"

"Why not?" my wife said.

"I mean, the woman is going to have a baby and she is up there *brushing her teeth?* A sudden surge of hormones is clouding her ability to reason. We'd better carry her out."

"Easy, pops," my son said.

Lisa came down the stairs, smiling and relaxed. "I'm ready," she said.

She glowed with a special radiance. Her teeth were blinding.

We made it to the hospital without problems. One o'clock in the morning isn't exactly the commute hour. Even in L.A. Traffic was light.

"I'll handle this," I said, as I pulled up to emergency.

A nurse came bustling out the door.

"Al Martinez," I said impressively, "L.A. Times."

I lowered my voice for impact.

"Fine, Elmer," she said, "you the mother?"

"Well . . . no."

"Where's the mother?"

My son helped Lisa from the car. "I'm the mother," Lisa said.

"Let's go, mama," the nurse said.

They put her in a wheelchair and hustled her away.

"Try to relax," my son called back.

"Come on, Elmer," my wife said. "We'll wait for the baby and later you can go home and play with your electric martini mixer."

"Man, I'm getting tired of everyone calling me Elmer."

Labor was fast. I barely had time to finish watching a Dean Martin movie, circa 1950, when Nicole was born.

What a wonder. A small, perfect life, kicking and wiggling. Hair the color of an amber sunset. Eyes that send you crashing through the ceiling.

Nicole.

What shall I tell you, my pretty? It's a world of grief and a world of pleasure, of high comedy and low motives, of a gold sheen on the ocean and armed jets in the sky. The wonders that await, Nicole. See them, dark eyes. Reach out for them, small hand.

"Well," my wife said, turning from the viewing window, "what do you think?"

"She's a beauty."

"Is that an objective journalistic assessment?"

"Precisely."

It was 3 o'clock in the morning.

"Come on, Elmer," she said. "I'll buy you a cup of coffee. Then we can go home and jump up and down on the dog."

I left with a backward glance.

Ah, Nicole. Ah, my lovely . . . .

— 30 —

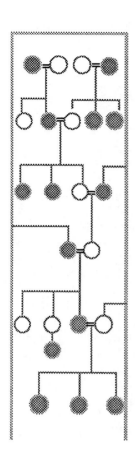

Rhythms
and
Rattles

"Ragaboon."

I have a friend named Nicole who is 5 months old, and sometimes we talk about things.

Well, actually, I do most of the talking because, at 5 months, you don't have a terrific vocabulary.

Nicole's favorite word, for instance, is "ragaboon," and while it is a fine word, possibly even the best word ever spoken, it is less than precise in its imagery.

I mention it, I suppose, not because of ragaboon itself but because of the way Nicole says it, touching my face, studying me with large hazel eyes, smiling suddenly with a glow that lights my life.

Ragaboon.

She said it to me the other day in a restaurant called the Hamburger Hamlet, which is where we dine occasionally.

The Hamlet is a kind of hangout for babies, and I like that. There are almost always infants around during the day and no one seems to mind when one of them begins to yowl.

Also, they make a very nice martini at the Hamlet. That is not their prime purpose, I suppose, else they would be known as the Martini Hamlet and not the Hamburger Hamlet.

However, I don't eat hamburgers because I am on a Pritikin diet and eat only eggplant cooked in rainwater. But I figure any place that can be kind to babies and still make a decent martini deserves mention here.

Martinis, by the way, are also not on the Pritikin diet, but I'm certain they will be someday as science defines their vast curative powers.

Nicole was crying when we sat down for lunch. Tears gleamed like diamonds on cheeks as soft as a summer whisper.

I hugged her and shook her rattle, which is a rhythm she usually responds to, but not this time. It's a red rattle with a smiling face.

I even tried baby talk, but I have never been too good at baby talk. I am a little better at it halfway through my first martini, but Nicole needed it right away.

In a matter of minutes, every baby in the restaurant was crying, because that's what babies do in a crowd. They have a kind of instinctive empathy with others of their kind, which is perhaps something we might think about.

I increased my efforts to calm Nicole, without much success. After several awkward attempts at *goo* and *gah* and *da-da-boo-boo,* I said, "What's the problem?"

She stopped crying suddenly and touched my face with her hand and said, "Ragaboon."

I thought about that.

What Nicole was telling me was that she was feeling sad because the year was ending and she hadn't accomplished everything she had intended.

I kissed her ear, which causes her to smile, and said, "You're only 5 months old, you can't expect too much from yourself."

"Ragaboon."

"I too have much I did not accomplish in 1986, but I did the best I could, and so did you. Be at peace with that, little one."

This caused me to think about how much time I had spent during the year doing nothing.

I am one of the world's two or three great amblers, drifting through life with a degree of aimlessness that is difficult to perceive.

I begin each day with great intentions, to go from here to there, to interview smartly, to write a column of wit and substance and then to go home and fix the broken kitchen drawer and take out the garbage and chat with my wife and still have an hour or so left to work on a movie.

But it's a fantasy world I create.

Because what really happens is that I begin to drift off my charted course and pretty soon I am on a dirt road somewhere, looking for a tree around the corner, or driving down a street I've never seen or staring at people from a coffee shop window.

Mostly it's the tree around the corner I seek, because I'm a tree freak and I could look at them forever, standing there like a mindless fool staring at the perfect symmetry of their branches and measuring the rhythm of the wind that moves them.

But then I wake up suddenly and say, *Damn you, Martinez, you've done it again, you've daydreamed away another day and you've still got a column to write and not an idea in your head and now what, muchacho?*

Good question.

I race to the office and work like a man on fire and vow never to do that again, but I will, no matter what I vow.

And then I go home, weary from the explosion of energy, and the kitchen drawer doesn't get fixed and the garbage doesn't get taken out and my wife, that poor woman, might as well be married to an aardvark. The movie script? Forget that too.

"The problem," I said to Nicole, "is that I get sidetracked. I start out striding and then forget about halfway through where I was going in the first place, so I amble off down a path and listen to the crickets."

"Ragaboon."

"I'm with you, kid. Next year, I knock their socks off. Next year, I go for the golden kazoo. Next year I fix the kitchen drawer."

She touched my face and I kissed her ear and we sat there for a very long time, Nicole with her rattle and me with my martini, wondering at the rhythms of the world and the tree around the corner.

— 30 —

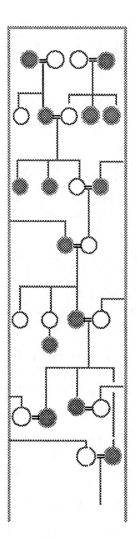

A
Shaky
Step
into
Scary Era

Thugs rule our streets
and fools run our govern-
ments, and the rest of us
struggle to survive in a
world beyond the looking
glass.

Into this, Nicole took her
first step . . . .

I have a friend named Nicole who is 11 months old and who took the first unassisted step in her life last week.

She hung tentatively to the tiniest edge of a coffee table, one small finger alternately touching and releasing the corner, and then with a courage we can only imagine, she walked.

It was not a long journey by the standard of miles she must trod down the years of her life, only a few unsteady steps across the golden tile. But oh, what a distance.

When she reached the window box that was her ultimate destination, she turned and flashed a smile as sweet as the first sunrise, holding it with an instinctive pride that wanted this moment in summer never to be forgotten.

I admit to a total lack of neutrality toward this dark-eyed girl who has entered my life with such light and warmth, and regard with special consideration whatever milestone she achieves on her journey from the cradle.

A step has special significance.

First words are less obvious to define, since babies seem to leap from the womb shouting *mama* and *dada,* and mothers are always prone to believe that *nagobodoodimyma* means energy equals mass times the speed of light squared.

In Nicole's case, that's probably true, but since she is no doubt saying it in Latin, I can't be sure.

A first step is a more obvious triumph, a visual motion toward the years ahead, a symbolic leap from the starting blocks, arms pumping, energy burning.

The image of that beautiful child standing proudly at her destination stayed with me throughout the day, and that night I tried to imagine where the first step might ultimately take my sunshiny Nicole.

It was after midnight and everyone was asleep.

I sat at my desk in a quiet house and shuffled through stories I had clipped from newspapers during the week, wondering how I

62

might measure Nicole's first step against an era fraught with special dangers.

They weren't clippings of major stories, not bloodstains on the Persian Gulf or the death of honor in Washington, but instances of more immediate peril in our own neighborhoods.

A young policeman murdered trying to stop a dope sale. A small boy killed in a drive-by shooting. A pit bull that savaged three innocent people. A prep school closed because its owner could no longer tolerate teen-age hostility. A Jewish temple desecrated with Nazi symbols.

Each incident isolated an area of danger Nicole must face as her first few steps grow to a dozen steps and the dozen to millions.

It won't be an easy journey.

Quiet rural neighborhoods have become war zones and our homes exist on perimeters of self-defense, bristling with dogs and weapons and alarms that scream like banshees in the night.

A disregard for life has become so acute that even drive-by shootings on the freeways of Los Angeles are a numbing reality, introducing random factors into urban assault that chill the blood.

We face a growing realization, perhaps not yet a fact, that schools aren't safe, parks aren't safe, neighborhoods aren't safe, freeways aren't safe, buses aren't safe, dogs aren't safe and even the kid next door is suspect.

A night walk invites disaster, an open window risks horror.

I'm not a philosopher and I'm not a social psychologist. I have no idea why violence grows and peril rides the winds. I can't remember when cocaine became a status symbol and gunfire a form of street-talk.

I only know, as a friend of mine says, that it's a distorted time in history, and ironies abound in a society that seems oddly out of sync.

Neighbors shout because a woman keeps a miniature horse in her yard, but silence greets the death of a small boy in a bloody drive-by.

Two young women are arrested for selling roses without a license in L.A. and Bernhard Goetz goes free after shooting four teen-agers in New York.

The homeless are pulled from the gutters of skid row only to complain about the dirt of the earth that surrounds their free tent homes.

Thugs rule our streets and fools run our governments, and the rest of us struggle to survive in a world beyond the looking glass.

Into this, Nicole took her first step, and I worry where the trail might lead.

I walked through the silent house and up the stairs to where she slept in her crib, an angel wrapped in the serenity of warmth and infancy.

How I wish there were ways I could shield her from the calamities of violence and protect her from the hounds of misfortune that bound through the back alleys of night.

But I have no magic to shape her future and no amulets to guard her life, so I kissed her gently on the cheek and climbed into my own bed.

I lay awake for a long time thinking about a little girl stepping tentatively across a sun-splashed floor, and then brooded over a moment in summer that couldn't last forever.

— 30 —

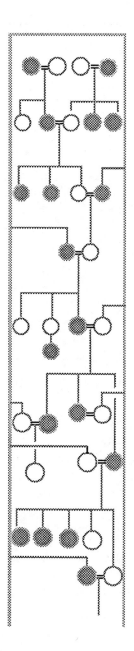

Dancing
With
the
Memories

More than 1 million
men, women and
children died on
both sides. Twice
that number were
mutilated.

It was the night of a storm. Rain drummed against the rooftops. Wind howled through the oak trees. Outdoor Christmas lights swung and blinked in the calamity, flicking spears of color at the massed energy of the weather.

Inside, a little girl named Nicole watched through a window as the gale swept leaves into the air and spun them like dust devils over the rain-damped wooden deck, *around and around and around . . . .*

The spinning leaves and swinging lights reflected in the windows and off the deck itself, creating in multiple dimension a kinetic fantasy of color, a dream scene that flickered and blinked like the neon of a child's imagination.

The magic was not lost on Nicole. At 17 months, she is still part of the mystery and movement that nature offers in grand display to the very young, taken by a little girl's willingness to fly with the storm.

So Nicole began to dance.

She twirled over the golden tile, arms outstretched, trying with a child's tenacity to equal the scale of breathlessness the night had achieved, stretching to meet the storm sounds, head back, eyes closed, sensing the softness of the rain, hearing the music of the wind.

I watched in fascination because this is a special child, and the wonder of her perceptions never cease to amaze me.

She seems somehow aware of my moods, patting me gently when I'm low, running at me when I'm up, as bright as sunrise, as quick as starshine.

But even comforted by the flow and whirl of this dancing sprite, my mood was heavy.

Christmas puts me in an uneasy frame of mind. It sweeps me back to a time of war when miracles were measured by the distance between life and a near-miss, when the music of the season was the whine and hiss of incoming shells.

I see mountainsides gleaming white under a bright moon and

hear the frozen air crackle with small-arms fire. I see blood the color of red ribbon stain the snow and hear cries of pain that resound to this day.

Korea, 1951.

A police action. A conflict that fell into a crack between two *real* wars. A war that Winston Churchill said couldn't be won, couldn't be lost and couldn't be ended.

More than 1 million men, women and children died on both sides. Twice that number were mutilated. There was so *much* anguish for so little recognition.

I thought of that as I watched Nicole dance before the storm, her own piquancy merged in reflection with the driving rain and the flashing colors, as different from war as laughter from pain.

She turned my way and smiled, and I returned the smile, but I couldn't get my mind off a Christmas in Korea a long time ago.

Names come to mind. Wertman, Citera, Mammaril, Landsford, Hopkins. Others emerge in memory as faces without names. A corporal from Ohio who smoked a pipe. A kid from Michigan who wanted to teach.

I saw them one Christmas in Korea when the battalion rested in reserve. We drank beer and shared packages and sang loudly in the camaraderie of young warriors, for a moment removed from the chaos that roared beyond the ridgeline.

By Jan. 1, most of them were dead.

The strands of life are thin. Bullets cut them. Mortars cut them. Land mines cut them.

Human flesh is no match for steel. One moment we sang, the next we mourned. I came to realize how transitory life could be in the complexities of battle and with what caprice war mocks our decencies.

Nicole danced through the memory, turning toward me occasionally to see if I were still watching, unaware how far away I had been in such a brief period of time.

Or *was* she unaware?

The rain lessened and the wind faded. The branches of the trees ceased to wave and the twirling leaves settled to the wet planking of the backyard deck. Strands of lights drooped motionlessly in the night.

The dance was over.

Nicole stopped spinning and observed the sudden silence. Then she turned to me. I was half-lying on a couch, still tense with the memories of war that wouldn't go away.

She came to my side, patted my leg and put her head down without saying a word. The connection had been made. She somehow understood.

Edna St. Vincent Millay wrote: "Childhood is the kingdom where nobody dies."

But it's more than that. Childhood is the kingdom where warmth exceeds passion and caring exceeds ego.

It's a place to dance without inhibition until the music fades, but to know that the music will come again someday, and the dance will continue.

"Nicole," I said to the little girl clutching my knee, "I really like you a lot."

She smiled and then was off in a flash, attracted by a new wonder in another room.

The enchantment had passed, but I know now I'll be able to close my eyes tonight and not see the faces of war that too often crowd my holidays.

I'll see a little girl spinning and twirling by storm-light, arms outstretched, head thrown back, reflected in every light that ever blinked at Christmastime.

It will be Nicole. She'll be dancing.

— 30 —

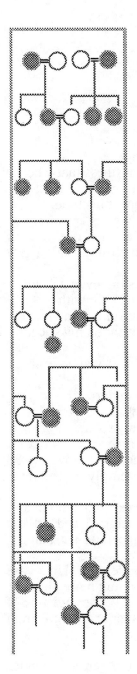

Time
on
My
Hands

I was cringing
against the fireplace
when I realized it was
out of plumb ...
Wait, maybe it isn't
the fireplace. The
wall! That's it, the
wall is crooked.

It is a tradition in the newspaper business that when a columnist returns from vacation he is entitled to waste at least one column discussing where he went and how he spent his time.

This is not because a columnist necessarily goes anywhere or does anything out of the ordinary but because when one returns from vacation, that thin margin of enthusiasm required to write a column in the first place has disappeared.

A columnist must therefore buy time to restore even a shadow of his prior motivation for doing what he does to begin with.

I say that by way of justifying today's cheerful but pathetic effort, because I am going to write about where I went on my vacation and what I did.

Where I went was nowhere and what I did was straighten things around the house.

This probably doesn't seem like a terrific undertaking to you, and it wasn't to me either until I spent three weeks at home and realized how many crooked things there were in every room.

To backtrack a little, the reason I stayed home was to work on a screenplay, but unless someone is standing next to me with a .38 against my head I am not likely to sit and write simply for the sheer spiritual joy of it.

So I wandered away from my word processor fairly often and watched television. While it was fun at first seeing Gary Hart and Jimmy Bakker trying to explain away their unzipped flies, that got boring very fast.

Actually, I shouldn't imply sexual impropriety in Hart's case because I don't *know* that he and Donna did anything more all night than discuss fund-raising techniques and possibly the logistics of transportation during a national political campaign based on Bimini Island.

That's what politics is all about.

After I wearied of electronic voyeurism I began to meander through the house. That's when I realized the couch was crooked.

"Funny," I said to my wife, "but I never noticed that before."

"Noticed what?"

"The crooked couch."

"Leave the couch alone."

"But it's at an angle," I said, kneeling to eye its position. "It should be more lined up with the lamp. Come to think of it, the lamp is crooked. The lamp should be lined up with the rose picture. Ho, ho, what's this? The rose picture . . . ."

"Stop!"

I had already straightened the couch and was about to move the lamp in preparation for straightening the rose picture when she picked up a vase, which was a little out of line anyhow.

Naturally I froze. My wife is essentially nonviolent but I have never been convinced that one of these days she might not whacko me.

"You are not," she said, "going to spend three weeks wandering through the house straightening things."

"I'm just trying to prevent disaster," I explained. "So much in the house is crooked that the place is in danger of tilting down the hill. We will be asleep some night and the cat will jump toward the north and that will be the infinitesimal shift in balance that will finally tilt our lovely little home over the precipice."

"Honest to God," she said, "you keep this up and no matter how much I love this vase I'm going to brain you."

I was cringing back against the fireplace when I suddenly realized it was out of plumb.

"Look," I said, pointing upward, "the damned thing flares outward at the top. No wonder the house fills with smoke. Wait, maybe it isn't the fireplace. The wall! That's it, the wall is crooked!"

She studied me for a moment then put the vase back on its stand.

"Sit down,"she finally said. "Here. On the crooked couch."

She sat next to me. Her voice was unusually calm.

"I love you," she said.

"Well, thank you. I love you too."

"But," she continued, putting a finger to my lips to shush me, "one of these days you are likely to retire. And I want you to know that if you spend your retirement wandering from room to room commenting on what's crooked and what's out of plumb, I'm going to have you killed."

"What?"

"I'm going to hire an ex-policeman or a Mafia hit man and have you rubbed out. Erased." She smiled very sweetly. "There are just certain things I won't take from you, Elmer. That's one."

"I see," I said, standing and looking around. "Well, I guess I'll get back to the old screenplay."

"That's a terrific idea. Work hard and I'll fix us a nice romantic dinner with maybe a bottle of your favorite white zinfandel and, after that, who knows?"

I smiled uneasily and went wandering toward my den when I noticed some lint on the rug. I picked it up and began looking around. I suddenly realized there was lint everywhere. In fact, I don't believe I have ever seen so much lint in my life.

But you know what? I didn't say a damned word about it, because there isn't a lint in the land that is worth my life.

I just went in there and began whacking away on the old word processor. The desk was a little crooked, but what the hell.

— 30 —

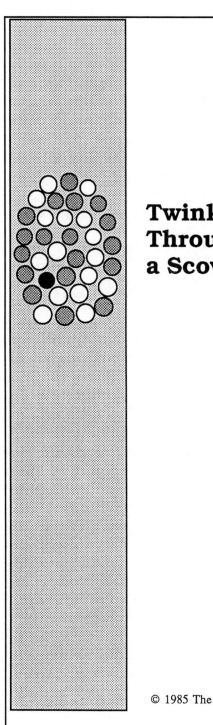

Twinkle
Through
a Scowl

"Hellit."

I have a very good friend named Travis who is 2 years old and who is going through a negative stage. I do not understand many of the stages of growing up and growing old. Mid-life, for instance, escapes me completely, and I don't ever remember being a teen-ager.

I do, however, understand the negative stage, since it is one, for God's own whimsical reasons, I have never grown out of. I therefore relate to Travis, and sometimes we wander up a trail in the Santa Monica Mountains together and shake our heads and say no and uh-uh and to hell with it.

Most people I know feel that I probably ought to encourage Travis to be more positive because he might not grow up to be a newspaper columnist and there are very few other occupations that require or will even tolerate a nature such as mine.

But these people do not understand the essential elements of the kind of negativity Travis and I embody. It is offered by my small friend, for instance, with a shrug and a smile and sometimes with a sound of laughter so sweet it is almost like music.

He says no with a twinkle, and, although I would rather cut out my tongue than twinkle, I realize that the nature of a no is often shaped by, if not a twinkle, a wry grin.

Travis and I discussed this the other day as we meandered along a trail that begins near my house in the Santa Monicas.

A light rain was falling and occasionally Travis would throw back his head and open his mouth to catch the moisture. I took his hand to guide him while he was thus involved and not watching the ground. It is a small hand, warm and trusting.

"The thing is," I said to him, "those of us who are negative are not easily understood by those who are positive, namely people with 'I Love God' bumper stickers on their modest Honda Civics."

"Nope," Travis replied.

"Being negative involves the ability to say the truth when the truth is not popular," I observed.

He said, "Uh-uh."

74

"Do you mean," I continued, as he turned around once to see if the rain would turn with him, "that you agree or disagree with me?"

"Hellit," Travis replied.

"We're going to have to work on that one," I said.

Travis is learning to talk quite well, but he seems to be having trouble saying to hell with it. We practice the phrase once in a while because I feel it is important for a negative person to be able to dismiss criticism with a cluster of words that are simultaneously negative, noncommittal and all-inclusive.

To hell with it does not single out any one group or even any one event, but summarizes a good-natured feeling of frustration and impatience with, well, everything.

"Are you *really* teaching him to say to hell with it?" Travis' mother asked one day, not quite believing that even I could stoop so low. Her name is Linda.

"Someone has to teach him," I said, "and it might as well be me. I am quite good at it actually."

Linda has known me for a very long time, so she just shook her head and smiled.

"Boy," I heard her say to her mother, "you really married a nut."

Meanwhile back on the trail:

"In terms of negative," I said to Travis, "you must . . . ."

"Nope," he interrupted.

"You have to wait until I'm finished, " I said.

He said nope again and no and hellit and shook his head and added "Mine!" which is his entire repertoire. Then he laughed, because he understood, that bright little boy, what a good joke he was playing on his old pal.

"Well," I said, "maybe you're right, Trav. Because, I guess, if you're conscious of your own negativism then you aren't really negative, are you?"

He threw his head back again to catch the rain in his mouth, tasting the place where storms are born. He closed his eyes and spread his arms at the same time. He was pretending he was flying, which shows a depth of wisdom difficult to find in one so young. He understood that the spirit soars when rain falls.

I mention this today only because, while searching about for a Thanksgiving Day column, I began to realize that I was awfully grateful to have Travis around. He has defined for me the nature of no in a manner that explains my own sour approach to life.

Travis catches rain in his mouth because rain is real, and he takes my hand because his trust is real. Words are bubbles that pop and disappear. No is a game people play.

"You're a very nice boy, Travis," I said, "and I'm terribly glad to have you around this Thanksgiving Day. I only wish everyone had someone as perceptive as you."

He laughed a laugh that enribboned the dark day with a light of its own. Then he shook his head no very, very hard, as hard as a boy of 2 can shake it, and he said, "Yes!"

I picked him up and hugged him and walked along the trail with Travis in my arms. His head was thrown back, his eyes were closed and his arms were outspread. We were flying.

— 30 —

ISSUES

On
an Autumn
Morning

...where a boy lay
dead of his own
raging quest....

The image remains fixed in my mind: a young man sprawled on his back by the side of the road on Topanga Canyon Boulevard, arms flung outward, eyes closed, his face gray-pallored and crimson-streaked, as though a makeup artist had applied these tones in a cinematic duplication of death.

But this was no movie, and there was no makeup, and the stillness that lay by the roadside was death in reality, final and unforgiving.

I came upon the scene moments after the man, flying down the canyon on a motorcycle, had lost control on a curve and gone head-on into an oncoming truck that batted him aside like a stuffed toy and bent his sports bike U-shaped.

There was no doubt in my mind as I slowed to offer help that the cyclist was dead, because I have seen that grayness often enough during 30 years of newspapering to recognize the pallor and to understand its meaning.

But I couldn't just drive by without at least some acknowledgement that a human life had ended. I stopped despite my foreboding.

A half-dozen others already stood awkwardly around the young man's body, like attendants at a funeral.

One of them, a woman, looked up as I approached and said paramedics had been called, and then she shook her head slowly as if to say it didn't matter anyhow; the boy was beyond paramedics.

Memories of sadness are often laced with contrast.

I recall, for instance, that the day was bright with an autumn sun, and the leaves of the liquid amber trees glowed in brilliant shades of red and yellow, trimming with painful iridescence a scene of somber grays.

I remember thinking that death had no business coming to one so young on a morning so vibrant with life.

I didn't write anything about the incident, though it continued to occupy a shadowy corner of my mind.

But I did begin gathering newspaper clippings of traffic fatali-

80

ties that involved motorcycles until they formed a kind of silent litany of grief in an envelope on my desk.

A speeding motorcyclist died when he failed to negotiate a curve . . . .

A motorcyclist was killed when he tried to ride between a truck and a bus . . . .

A man died after his speeding motorcycle struck a van . . . .

A man was killed when his motorcycle slammed head-on into a pickup . . . .

A man died when he rode his motorcycle at high speed into the back of a truck . . . .

Then an incident occurred so like the one I had witnessed that it was as though the scene was being replayed in a pattern doomed to repeat itself as long as the young seek speed.

A motorcyclist died on Topanga Canyon Boulevard when he swerved out of his lane and went head-on into a van in almost the same area where death took the young man of my own nightmares.

Was there a pattern here? Had I been noticing more motorcycle fatalities only because of the one seared into memory, or were there actually more occurring?

Both.

True, I can't get that image of death by a roadside out of my mind. But it is also true that statewide the number of motorcyclists killed on the highways has doubled in the past 10 years.

I asked a highway patrolman what was happening.

"Simple," said Officer Craig Klein. "Motorcycles are getting faster, and there are more of them on the road.

"Some can do 150 miles an hour. They go from zero to 100 in the blink of an eye. The machine is outdoing the capabilities of its riders."

Topanga Canyon, he said, is a special problem. Sports cyclists use the twisting, two-lane boulevard as a race track, revving up to speeds far exceeding a level of sanity required for driving *anything* on the 12-mile stretch between the valley and the ocean.

"They try passing on the wrong side of the road and end up as statistics," Klein said. "Last year there were three motorcycle accidents within a few days that all involved head-on collisions. Two of them were fatal.

"When these 500-pound machines are operated by someone who doesn't know what he's doing, they become unguided missiles."

I've never liked motorcycles. The vulnerability of bikers in mixed traffic is beyond acceptable risk. What otherwise would constitute minor injuries become fatalities in the simplest collisions between bike and car or bike and almost anything else.

It's a lousy way to die.

I have argued ad nauseam with those who tell me I don't understand the freedom of wind in my face and roaring horsepower between my legs, and maybe they're right. They say I have outlived a quest for speed, and maybe they're right there too.

But therein lies an irony, that these machines of rush and power are primarily playthings of the young, and the young are least emotionally equipped to handle their deadly potential.

Testaments to the risks youth is willing to take for the sake of its own incandescence exist daily, but nothing is worth that autumn scene by the roadside, where a boy lay dead of his own raging quest to get there a microsecond sooner.

— 30 —

Three Guys Talking About Death

**Who killed
Mark Miller?**

Who killed Mark Miller?
Not I, says the kid with the gun. It was a mistake, an accident.
Not I, says the father. I warned him about drinking, I warned him about gangs.
Not us, say the teen discos. We watch them while they're here.
Not us, say the police. Parents aren't supervising their kids.
Not us, say the media. We only report the news.
Not I, says the rabbi. Teen-agers are losing respect for life.
Not I, says the city. It's a violent age, we do the best we can.
Then who killed Mark Miller?

We are at the Shemrun Cafe, having a few drinks, on an evening as sweet and warm as hot buttered rum. There is me and Scott and a guy I've never met before, a skinny kid from Jersey named Cobalt, who is a friend of Scotty's. We are talking about Mark Miller.

I've known Scotty for a few years so I am aware that violence isn't his favorite subject. He would rather talk about women or politics or the Dodgers. Anything but mayhem.

They say he got that way after Vietnam, and I usually respect his wishes. But this time it's different

I can't get Mark Miller out of my mind.

Here is a kid, just 15, who gets p.o.'d because another 15-year-old musses up the *purple* hair of his girlfriend at a teen-age disco. They fight about it, get thrown out of the club and you'd think that would be that. But it isn't.

The kids meet again a few days later in the disco's parking lot. The fight resumes, and, in a twinkling of the time it took him to be born, Mark Miller is dead. Within hours, the other kid, the one they call Chris, is an accused killer.

"How can a thing like that happen?" I ask. "Two boys in a lousy fight over some girl's punk-style *purple* hair! A bullet in the head defending . . . *nothing!*"

84

No one says anything for a moment. The commute traffic has thinned on Topanga Canyon Boulevard and there aren't many customers in Shemrun, so we sit in mostly silence.

Then Scotty finally says, "It's the age. Purple hair, a disco for teen-agers, dope, gangs. All those things."

"Purple hair," I say, shaking my head. "I mean, it's like a scene from 'Clockwork Orange.' I see a girl in whiteface with purple hair and brilliant green lipstick and then these two guys in black and white . . . ."

"Look," Scotty says, interrupting, "the girl didn't do it. Purple hair's a style. Fads don't kill people."

Cobalt is sitting there all this time staring at his Scotch and water, saying nothing. Lights from behind the bar reflect in his round, silver-rimmed glasses.

"Something besides a kid pulled that trigger," I say. "Kids didn't kill kids when I was a teen-ager. There are forces loose we don't understand."

We are on our second drink. I tend to get metaphysical after one. I see life in surrealistic terms, distorted and mysterious.

"People die," Scotty says. He is growing uneasy with the subject. "It happens all the time. War, murder, traffic accidents. . . . I knew a guy in 'Nam who lived a charmed life. Three different times he should be killed, but each time he barely misses death. So he comes home and you know what he does? He shoots himself in the head."

"Why?" I ask.

"Who can figure it?" Scotty says. "Some people have the *look* of death. You can see it in their eyes."

"Did your pal in Vietnam have the look?" I ask.

Scotty nods his head slowly. "He had it all right. I knew it the first day I saw him."

Then suddenly he slams a fist so hard on the table that our glasses jump. "Why in the hell are we talking about this?"

"Because it exists."

For a moment I think it is someone at another table talking, but then I realize it is Cobalt. He lifts his head from staring at his drink and looks to me and then to Scotty, who by now has had it with the whole evening.

"You guys solve the Cock Robin question," Scotty says. "I'm splitting."

He is out the door before I can calm him down. Cobalt is nodding thoughtfully.

"Who killed Cock Robin?" he says mostly to himself. Then he focuses on me. "You want to know who killed that kid in the Valley?"

I shrug noncommittally.

Cobalt leans in close. "Rambo did it," he says.

I am staring at the guy, not quite knowing how to respond, when I notice he has yellow eyes. I have known only one other person with yellow eyes, and he was crazier than hell.

"Rambo?" I finally say, careful not to upset him.

"Our love of guns," Cobalt says, "our glorification of violence, our rituals of blood, our fascination with death. They go by the name *Rambo!*" He arcs his hand through the air and almost whispers, "Up there, on the silver screen."

Then he's gone.

I sit there for a long time, thinking. *Rambo in his camouflaged dungarees and combat boots, a dark sweatband around his forehead, armed to the teeth, stalking through the jungles, shooting, slashing.*

"You know," I say to a guy passing, "maybe old Yellow Eyes is right. Maybe Rambo did it."

"Whatever you say, pal."

That's what I say.

— 30 —

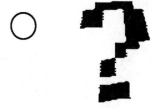

Notes
From
a Citadel
of Lerning

What we're dealing
with are journalism
students who don't
read newspapers.

For those eagerly awaiting the next generation of journalists to improve the sorry lot of today's newspapers, I bear grim tidings. They can't spel and they think Desmond Tutu is a ballerina.

That may not mean a lot out there, since good spelling is not a requirement for pumping gas or repairing furnaces, but to those of us in the business of accurate information, an ability to spell is, to say the least, essential.

Similarly, you might ask who gives a rat's whisker about Desmond Tutu, and I reply that, while you don't care, we ought to. If nothing else, Des may perform someday at the Music Center and we may be called upon to cover his act.

But rather than debate that which you obviously know very little about, I offer proof of the sad state of today's California journalism students. Weep along with me.

It all began with a test of 100 undergraduates at Cal State Fullerton. Sixty percent of them didn't know who Alexander Hamilton was, while 60% *did* know who Erika Kane was.

(Erika Kane, I will tell you, is a soap opera character, but I'll be damned if I'll tell you who Alexander Hamilton is. Look it up.)

The students were similarly ignorant of Geoffrey (Jeff) Chaucer and Mikhail Gorbachev, the main characters on television's old "Man from U.N.C.L.E." series, and Dante Alighieri, the Italian gymnast.

Obviously appalled by this, a teacher at Cal State Northridge gave the same test to 44 undergraduates and was delighted that, at least, a lesser percentage knew who Erika Kane was. Teaching, I suppose, has some triumphs, however dwarfish they may appear.

While looking into this, I came upon a journalism instructor who each week gives her students a quiz of current events, news being an area of interest one would expect to find among journalism students.

An element of the test was a requirement to spell California Gov. George Deukmejian's name. Of 15 students, only two spelled it correctly, three who obviously knew him personally called him "Duke" and the others tried with Deukmagien, Dekmajan, Dukemagen and so on.

Well, I hear you cry, it's a difficult name to spell, and I agree. But it isn't exactly a little-used or unfamiliar name in California, and since these are California journalism students and he is, like it or not, the governor, one would assume the majority would get it right, right?

The same for Nancy Regan and Lt. Gov. Leo Mckarthe and Mayor Tom Bradly, names that they also managed to boot all over the campus.

Incidentally, in another test, nine out of 14 had never heard of U.S. Atty. Gen. Edwin Meese while 13 out of 14 knew that a California teen-ager was not chosen for her high school cheerleading squad because her breasts were too large.

"It's both funny and sad," the teacher said. She asked not to be identified. "What we're dealing with are journalism students who don't read newspapers. In a question on the prior week's news, one said a B-52 had overflown SALT II. He thought it was a geographic area.

"Questions involving history are also lost on most of them," she said, "especially recent history. Some, for instance, believe Jacqueline Kennedy Onassis to be the mother of U.S. Sen. Ted Kennedy." Close but no cigar.

The teacher added somewhat wistfully: "They have to be among the top third of the students in their high schools to get into a state university. I can't help but wonder about the other two-thirds."

One must understand, I suppose, that these are, after all, young people and it is difficult to divert their attention away from sex and beer in order to get them to concentrate on the dynamics of social change.

Who cares, for instance, about the fate of the "Diary of Anne Frank" in Greenville, Tenn., (obviously a hard porn flick banned at local theaters) when there is a prospect of getting drunk and laid after tonight's party? First things first.

All right. I was young once, though not for long, and can well understand the intensity of an undergrad's interest in passions other than those found down the cool corridors of academia.

But you'd think that, since they *know* they're going to get the same basic test every week, they'd at least study for it, a process by which one reads and thinks about major items relative to one's field of interest.

What bothers me, I guess, is not so much dumb journalism students but what appears to be a growing disregard for the basic tools of communication, i.e. knowledge and the ability to transmit that knowledge beyond grunts and mumbles.

But, what the hell, with Ronald Reagan running the country and Sylvester Stallone defining the new American Syntax, sex and beer may, after all, be the destiny of the mind, and probably ought to be encouraged wherever college students gather.

So bottoms up in both instances, kids, and the devil take tomorow. I mean tomorrow.

— 30 —

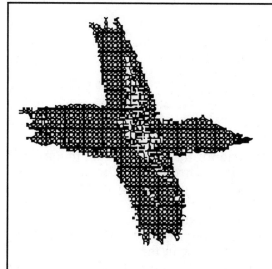

A
Faint
and Eerie
Rustling

The face haunted
her, so she bought
a shotgun. It cost
$129.

She has lived alone for the past 18 years in a modest home in the San Fernando Valley, surrounded by memories: Pictures of a husband who died in his sleep on a rainy night in October. A chipped gold-plated baseball trophy from a son who now lives in Chicago. An afghan from a daughter in Oregon.

The small living room glows faintly from the single light of a table lamp, leaving patches of shadow in the corners. The drapes are tightly drawn, shutting out what remains of the fading day. The room is cast in the colors of the past, sepia-toned, amber-tinted.

As I enter her home, I am struck not so much by the somber nature of the room as I am by the harsh, metal lines of its newest addition.

Mary Crawford owns a shotgun.

It stands propped against a dark-wood piano that divides entryway from living room, in clear view of anyone at the door. She makes no reference to the weapon as she leads me in, turning down the sound of the old Sylvania television set. Its picture plays in silence.

She had been watching the news. And the news these days is of a man they call the Night Stalker.

"I have some root beer," she says, disappearing for a moment into a kitchen to the right of the living room. Her voice comes to me as I settle in an easy chair her husband once favored. "It's Hires."

In a moment she emerges with two full glasses. The burden seems almost too great and I find myself wondering how an old lady who can barely lift two glasses of root beer is ever going to be able to fire a shotgun.

She sits across from me and smiles, and then allows me into her terror.

Mary Crawford isn't her real name. She makes me promise I will disguise her identity and insists on approving the name I use. Crawford is as good as any.

She is 76 years old. Her back is bent from a mugger's assault a decade ago. A young man beat her senseless when she refused to give up her purse.

The attack left her in terror of the night, imprisoned by the fear that the mugger could strike again. He was out there, she knew, crouched in a doorway, hiding behind a wooden fence at the corner, waiting in the shadows of a pepper tree.

"And now this," she says, gesturing toward the silent television set. She stares at the newscasters for a moment, certain they are discussing the Night Stalker. "My God," she says.

We also call him the Valley Intruder. He strikes in the silent, eerie time before dawn, killing and raping, a composite face in the blurred horror of the attack, thin-lipped, wild-eyed.

Mary Crawford is certain she has seen him. So are hundreds of others who, like Mary, have telephoned the police. Sheriff Sherman Block says, "There's a killer out there."

"He was in a car in the parking lot at Vons," Mary remembers. "He stared at me, then was gone Jimminy Cricketts." She indicates with a gesture the speed of his departure.

The face haunted her, so she bought a shotgun. It cost $129. Mary lives on Social Security and on what her son and daughter send her occasionally. The shotgun is a sacrifice.

I prod gently. Has she ever fired one before? No. Has she ever fired any weapon? No. I doubt that she can, either physically or psychologically. Victims face immense odds. Decent people find it difficult to cause pain. Madmen don't.

Mary sips at her root beer. Every painful movement emphasizes age and frailty. I picture her alone, a large gray cat curled up at the foot of her bed. The cat's head jerks up suddenly, listening. Hands reach through a partly opened window . . . .

"I have never slept too well," Mary Crawford is saying. *Has she read my thoughts?* "Now I don't sleep at all."

The poet Acrisius wrote, "To him who is in fear, everything rustles." Shadows form faces. A breeze whispers the hushed footfall of a maniac. *Something's out there, something's coming . . . .*

Mary telephoned me when there seemed no one else to call. The police were checking. Neighbors were busy. Grown children were far away.

I can offer little solace but to say that an army of detectives is searching for the Night Stalker. Of 8 million people in the county, the immense likelihood is she will not be a victim.

But still . . . .

"Have you ever been afraid?" she asks, smiling slightly from embarrassment.

"Yes," I say, remembering the war in Korea. "But we learn to live with our fears."

"It isn't fair," she says.

The news breaks for a commercial. Youth dances across the screen in silent pirouette. Strong muscles flex and tense, smiles dazzle.

"No, it isn't," I say.

The world rustles around us. Old ladies listen. Eyes widen, hearts pound. *Have we come down the years to twilight for this? Have we weathered the hard days only to fear the gentle nights?*

I can't answer.

The most I can do, Mary Crawford, is ponder the madness that brings terror like a dream-sound into our quiet homes, and to feel sadness beyond measure that sometimes the faint and haunting rustle in the darkness is real.

— 30 —

On a Bus Bound for Nowhere

Peace on earth, good will toward who?

You remember Christmas. It was that brief period last December when the milk of human kindness fairly bubbled from our ears, so high was the level of charity stewing around in our Christian souls.

You remember the homeless. They were the people we erected tents for during Christmas, the derelicts we fell all over ourselves to feed, the new poor we paraded around town in holy tribute to our perfect rectitude.

We took them into our homes and crammed them full of turkey, cried over their calamities and vowed in voices choked with emotion that the time had come to bring the spirit-battered flotsam of an affluent society back ashore.

But that was December, and this is March.

The striped tents on the lawns around City Hall have long since been struck, and so has the rhetoric of beneficence that flapped like a yellow banner in the shifting breezes of Christmas caprice.

Peace on earth, good will toward who?

The homeless just aren't popular anymore. It's out of style to give a damn about the 30,000 or so human beings without a place to go or a meal to eat who drift like lost children through the streets and canyons of L.A.

Get a job. Get a haircut. *Get ahold of yourself!* Go away.

Consider the case of the Fiesta Motel.

It's an unimposing place amid car shops and fast-food restaurants on North Hollywood's Lankershim Boulevard, a street less noted for elegance than tedium. The neighborhoods flanking the thoroughfare are downward modest. The motel fits in.

Since the first of the month, the Fiesta has made 20 rooms available to the homeless under a plan funded by the federal government. Each person gets a $15-a-day voucher for a temporary place to stay. No one gets rich.

It was owner Leslie Goldhammer's idea. He knew what it was like to be homeless. A Hungarian Jew, he had many relatives who died in Nazi concentration camps during World War II. Goldhammer lived by hiding and running. No home of his own and nothing to eat.

At war's end, he came to this country, worked hard and ended up on the high side of society. Now he wants to give something back. But the neighbors around the Fiesta are fighting him.

They say the program is importing addicts, drunks and thieves. Stan Goldhammer, the owner's son, says that's a lie.

Ninety percent of those on vouchers are women and children, he angrily insists. "We could fill the place every night with bums and crooks, but we've eliminated them to provide for the homeless. Is this what happens when you try to help?"

I talked with the Fiesta's neighbors on Stagg Street, down Blythe, along Simpson.

"Nobody wants homeless people around here," a 300-pound machinist said. He greeted me shirtless and ate meat with his fingers from a plate on a coffee table. Thick rolls of fat gird his middle. "We don't want no trash."

"They're hardened drifters," a bleached-blonde manicurist said. A cigarette just crushed still burned in an ashtray. She lit another. "If they were just old, OK, but they're not. They're off the streets." Her eyes burned with anger. "They're tougher than hell."

"I don't want them anywhere *near* me," a man in his undershirt said from behind a screen door clogged with dust. A baby cried somewhere in the house. He shouted for it to shut up. "They're filthy bums," he said. The door slammed shut.

It was that way. Put 'em in jail. Put 'em in the poorhouse. Put 'em on a bus bound for nowhere. *Just get them out of here.*

What they'd like is a breed of homeless who are clean and quiet. Decent folks in pressed coveralls and gingham dresses temporarily down on their luck but working hard to rise above the gnawing guilt of their own inadequacies.

A middle-aged woman said to me that, if the homeless believed in God, they wouldn't be homeless. God provides for the good, doesn't he? "Shame on them!" she said.

We are an imperfect species. The derelicts among us are even less perfect. Didn't we know that last Christmas? They're a sad and tortured element of society, strangled by their own misery, paralyzed by the awesome requirements of simply getting started.

Rising from bed is a challenge, working an effort, succeeding an impossibility.

There may be junkies among them. Drunks, too. Poverty saps

the spirit and kills the visions that shape a man's tomorrows. Dreams provide the psychic energy required to galvanize the soul. Without dreams, the only escape is down a path blurred by booze and drugs, where being you doesn't hurt as much.

The neighbors around the Fiesta Motel may well succeed in ending the program Les Goldhammer initiated to provide for the homeless. But it won't matter. All those thieving bums and hungry women and shabby kids have to do is hang on for another nine months.

There'll be turkey all around at Christmas time. And enough Christian charity to make you wonder just where in the hell it all goes the day the tree comes down.

— 30 —

Getting
a Kick Out
of Killing

War is exciting,
creates a sense of
camaraderie, offers
the opportunity
for a good tan.

It's a great year for war buffs. The 10th anniversary of the Vietnam War, the 40th anniversary of World War II, the 140th anniversary of the Civil War and the 2,130th anniversary of the Third Punic War. Nostalgia flows like honey for the good old days.

There were other wars, of course, but their anniversaries fall between the traditional 10-year milestones we have adopted in America to commemorate battles of the past. And so we ignore them until their decades roll around.

Meanwhile, however, everyone is having a good time remembering, when possible, their nights in the foxholes and in the jungles and arguing about which war was, well, *best*. Only the Civil and the Punic wars are getting short shrift since there are no veterans around to join in the fun.

I feel, in view of the prevailing attitude, that I ought to say something positive about war since this isn't the time to be an old fuddy-duddy (do they still say that?) and remind everyone that when a war is actually *happening* it doesn't seem all that terrific. At least, mine didn't.

But what the hell, I said to myself, you can't have everything, right? So why not scratch up a few words that might contribute to the general mood of enjoyment that seems to be encouraging a festive attitude among the war fans of America.

So how's this: War is exciting, creates a sense of camaraderie and offers the opportunity for a good tan.

Those aren't actually my words, but the words of Ross Alexander, a nonviolent, anti-war, ex-hippie who is making money inviting grown men to shoot at each other with paint-pellet guns in what appears to be mock killing but which Ross insists is a sport.

Alexander runs an organization called Skirmish Inc. Each weekend in a field near Westlake Village, he arms eager yuppie sportsmen with cattle-marking guns, goggles and face paint and sets them loose to play an updated version of Capture the Flag.

But it isn't a war game, Ross said to me the other day in his hillside home. Well, yes, participants wear camouflaged dungarees and, well, yes, they do shoot at each other, but even so, you can't call it war.

Those marked by a paint pellet, for instance, aren't killed, he explained, but *eliminated,* a euphemism with limits of its own but, I suppose, still better than a bullet between the horns. For one thing, you don't bury eliminatees.

Later the young bankers and producers and lawyers gather around their Porsche Targas and BMWs to drink beer and compare strategies, accompanied, no doubt, by man-laughter and friendly punches to the arm.

"They're like little boys playing," Ross' wife, Carol, observed affectionately. She is anti-war, anti-gun, pro-nuclear freeze and not too crazy about football, but has come to understand that Skirmish is all just a bunch of fun.

"It doesn't perpetuate hostility," she said. "On the contrary, it may be a relief."

"Right," Ross agreed. "A safety valve for office tensions."

It was then he explained how the game of war, I mean sport of skirmishing, creates that sense of camaraderie after a day of excitement in the sun. "Gets the old adrenalin pumping," was the way he put it.

What I've done, you see, is apply Ross' enthusiasm for the sport to actual warfare in order to create a positive stance toward what we're celebrating in 1985.

War, let's face it, does offer its participants an abundant share of thrills and chills, most of it is outdoor work and, depending upon the climate, affords an excellent opportunity for an even tan. In that sense, I suppose, it isn't too different from, say, tennis.

And camaraderie is certainly an important link among men whose very lives might depend on the guy next to them. Unlike Ross Alexander's sport, where one can simply shout "paint check" to stop the action, real war offers no such verbal haven to those in trouble, or those in pain.

Only a strangled cry for medic even comes close.

But, hey, listen, I'm not here today to poop the party sweeping the country, and I'm not here to inhibit anyone's efforts to make a little money. I think Ross and Carol are already troubled enough by the compromises they must make in order to live with an uneasy gimmick and don't need me dancing around their conscience.

Call it what you will, war games or sport, the inclination for posturing young men to dress up in battle clothes and shoot at each other is the result of a national pathology that causes us to celebrate what we ought to abhor.

But, darn, there I go again, as old Ron Reagan might say, spittin' on the drums that call us to the party, stumbling in my attempt to march with tolerable good humor toward where the war buffs play.

I guess, thinking back on all of it, to nights of terror and cries of agony, to young men reduced to crimson tangles of flesh and bone, to the blood (not paint) of friends spattered on my face, I never did have a lot of fun at war.

But there I go again.

— 30 —

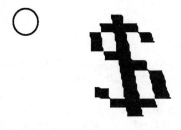

Let's Make a Deal

Everything is for sale in America, so why not grades.

I have always enjoyed working near a large university, not because of the glow of learning that lights the campus but because universities are so often in foment.

Hardly a year passes that someone doesn't want to burn a bra, a book or an effigy for an outrage that at first offends the academic spirit but then is forgotten by the spring break, when the collective concentration wanders from righteous cause to beer and sex.

I have been privileged over the past few years to report on two of the righteous causes that briefly captured the general interest and thus splashed beyond their puddle of origin at Cal State Northridge into the outside world.

One was a student feminist attempt to abridge the First Amendment by outlawing girlie magazines on campus. It was more an exercise in training-bra polemics than serious social warfare, shaping noisy young women for future feminist engagements in the grown-up world. When the smoke cleared, their effort lay in shambles and the vision of Thomas Jefferson remained secure.

The second issue encompassed anonymous accusations of sexual harassment of female students by male teachers, trailing dark rumors of quid pro quo exchanges involving sex and grades. The matter received wide attention but was ultimately resolved, as almost everything is, when a campus committee was appointed to study the problem.

Meanwhile, I'm pleased to report, a new crisis has reared its preppy head at Cal State, which is to say the alleged selling of grades by two faculty members in the Pan-African Studies Department. This, at least, has nothing to do with sex but simply involves good old American enterprise.

The two faculty members are accused of having promised A grades to students who sold 20 raffle tickets that would benefit a nonprofit foundation headed by one of the professors. The tickets sold for $5 each. Many of the students, I am told, were simply buying the tickets themselves which, in effect, meant they were buying

104

an A for $100. Bs, one student said, went for 15 raffle tickets or $75.

Three classes were canceled as a result of the revelation and the two faculty members are crying innocent with the same emotional fervor that Ollie North employed to elevate disgrace to a level of national heroism. One of the professors even implied that selling raffle tickets as a class project was meant to help shy students overcome their social timidity.

University spokespeople, meanwhile, are attempting to communicate the seriousness of what they call a "breach of educational standards." A vice president said that selling tickets for a raffle is not a "legitimate instructional activity" and suggested there were "sufficiently serious irregularities to raise doubts of educational relevance."

For those unaccustomed to academic argot, that means somebody screwed up.

I'm probably not as shocked and appalled as I ought to be. If the charges are true, the professors, in fact, demonstrated a unique application of the free-market spirit. Everything is for sale in America, so why not grades? Buying a university degree is no worse than buying one's way into heaven and would certainly alleviate the crowded conditions higher education is forced to endure.

One undergrad pointed out that the main attraction of the for-sale A was that you didn't have to go to class. Apply this across the board. If grades were made generally available for a price, a student who wanted a degree without the boredom of study could simply mail a check in and go about his slothful way, thus opening our classrooms to those with a more traditional, though certainly less imaginative, outlook.

One could perceive this as a form of deregulating America's universities, a condition of which Ronald Reagan would most certainly approve after consulting Nancy and the stars.

More students in the end would receive graduate degrees and this in itself would raise America's esteem in the eyes of the world, statistically at least. Imagine being able to boast that 82% of our students have bachelors' degrees, 72% have MAs and 63% are Ph.D.s.

Fair and equitable price structures would have to be established, of course, to ensure that a level of consistency, if not quality, is maintained. What I'm saying is you won't be able to buy an A in business ethics for the same low price you'd pay for an A in aerobics. This is no flea market, baby.

Courses of study which ultimately would lead to positions in more lucrative fields such as personal injury law might even be limited to the highest bidders, thus assuring that our better professions would not be cluttered by those of dimmer social eclat.

I envision a brave new era for academia and, at last, a nation of people able to achieve their grandest goals armed not with a head full of esoteric knowledge, but with simple proof of purchase.

If that doesn't save our universities, I wouldn't worry too much. The Japanese will probably buy them someday anyhow.

— 30 —

Sunrise
on a
Toxic Sea

**"I've been
fishing off
this pier since
1942. I know
these fish."**

Early morning fog lay over the ocean like strands of silver ribbon when Jake began fishing from the Santa Monica Pier. He seemed a part of both the fog and the sea, at 6-feet-4 a towering and square-jawed man of 75 with thick white hair and a tanned and weathered face.

"You've got to *fish* for the halibut," Jake was saying, moving his pole in wide, smooth circles. "They sure as hell ain't going to come to you."

There was a gentle gruffness to his tone, a combination peculiar to big men aware of their size, and old men aware of the ironies.

"I've been fishing off this pier since 1942," Jake said. "I know these fish." He laughed loudly. "Nobody knows 'em like old Jake."

His full name is Jake Spitzer. He comes to the pier three or four times a week early in the morning, before the crowds, almost always wearing a faded blue jump suit that accentuates his proportions. He weighs 207 pounds and, age notwithstanding, still looks as though he could clean out a saloon full of bullies without spilling a drop of beer.

I came looking for fishermen that gold and silver morning to test attitudes. Toxicologists are saying Santa Monica Bay has been poisoned by chemicals, and that the fish are time bombs of cancer. Carcinogens like DDT, cyanide and PCBs. I wanted to know how the fishermen felt.

It was too early for the crowds. The beach belonged to the sea gulls, dipping and soaring in full flight over the sand, calling to each other across the quiet morning.

Pier concessions were just opening. Delivery trucks came and went. In a parking lot below, a film crew prepared to shoot a shampoo commercial.

A half-dozen fishermen leaned over the rails around Jake, waiting for the first faint tug that signaled a catch, their lines moving to the gentle rhythms of the surf, pulled inward, flowing back. One man stood apart, not fishing, staring at the water.

"I used to fish here," he said, "but no more. I wouldn't eat any of that stuff now." He was in his mid-30s and wore a gray running suit. "But I guess it really doesn't matter, does it? The rain is acid and the air's polluted, so why worry about a few poisoned fish?"

Bob Carvel eats the fish. Not the junk fish—the herring and the Santa Monica croaker. "But the halibut's OK," he said. "The halibut's a migratory fish, it doesn't live in the bay." He moved his pole from side to side. "I eat the halibut."

After a moment he added defensively, "Everything's got DDT in it." Pause. "But not the halibut."

Jake Spitzer fished off the end of the pier. He laughed loudly at the very notion that someone would not eat the fish because of reports from college people. College people have nothing to do *but* report. His laugh was as large as the man, full-throated and challenging.

"That Filipino next to me," he said, gesturing toward a dark-skinned man, "hell, he eats it all. He don't throw nothing away. You'd have to eat 10 pounds of fish a day for the rest of your life to get cancer."

Jake laughed again, visualizing someone eating 10 pounds of fish a day. Fish for breakfast, lunch and dinner, fish on Sundays as well as Wednesdays. "You'd throw up before you got cancer!" He was still chuckling as he moved his pole in circles. It seemed no larger than a pencil clutched in a fist the size of a pot roast.

When Jake isn't at the pier, he tends gardens. His own and three others. Life is too short to watch it fade out of reach from a rocking chair. A rocking chair is an open casket waiting to be filled.

On fishing days he stops at the Venice Canal first for the fiddler crabs and moss he uses as bait.

"You want to see something dirty," he said, "you look at *that* place. I watch people catch clams that are black as night. I wouldn't eat the damned things, but they don't care. They eat it all. Maybe they eat the shells too, eh?"

"Look at the water here how nice and green. Would it be nice and green if it were polluted? No!" A big fist slammed down on the railing. "I give most of the fish away. I wouldn't give it to people to eat if it were poisoned.

"I tell 'em to put a little batter on it and fry it in a low heat so it won't burn."

What bothers Jake most is that the pier has not been restored since winter storms three years ago tore away 400 feet jutting into the ocean.

"They're always moaning about money," he said. "Why don't they fix the damned thing and put it out there where it was? Then we'd catch *fish*. That's the trouble," he added thoughtfully. "They don't care. No one cares."

I wondered. Do they care? Do they *really* care? Not just about the pier. Do they care about the acid rain, the polluted air, the poisoned sea?

Human priorities are ranked according to cost. Posterity is without measure and therefore lacks position on the chart. Tomorrow is a dream. Chemistry is real.

Jake was still grumbling about the pier when I left. A woman with three young boys had been standing to one side, listening. As I passed, she smiled faintly and said, "What are they doing to us?"

"I wish I knew," I said.

Morning was in full blossom. The fog was burning away. Santa Monica Bay glistened in the sunlight.

— 30 —

Sex,
Mom,
School
and
Apple
Pie

What once seemed easy now seems out of control. We can't supply answers because we're still working on the questions.

The Los Angeles school board, in an effort to discourage teen-age pregnancy, wants to establish a kind of model high school birth-control cafeteria where one might, if one wishes, obtain contraceptives with the ease of buying a tuna salad sandwich and a cup of chicken soup.

The board's vote was 6 to 1 and has instantly divided just about everyone into two categories: those who believe in God and those who do not believe in God. Those who believe in God are naturally opposed to the clinic and those who do not believe in God support it. That may seem like a simplification, but then that's what I do, simplify.

Barely 2 days old, the idea of establishing what some are calling a campus sex clinic already has transcended secular debate into that loftier arena where the futures of humanity and morality are determined.

What the school board wants to do basically is stop teen-age pregnancy. One way to stop it, as everyone knows, is to keep the kids from engaging in that activity most likely to result in the female of the pair becoming great with child.

But, short of beating them with a broom or drenching them with a hose at the height of their sexual aerobics, that's not an easy task. Young boys who will not lift a finger to rake the lawn will swim nine miles through alligator-infested swamps to reach a girl with a willing way.

So the school board decided that, since kids are going to do it anyhow, they might as well learn how to do it right. By *right* I mean how to do it without becoming pregnant, not how to do it better.

Sex education, into which category a clinic would probably fall, started becoming a question of prime importance sometime in the 1950's, when sex was discovered in a small laboratory near the Berkeley campus of the University of California.

I remember thinking at the time that, although sex seemed like a fine new pastime, it probably ought to be discussed in a clinical environment rather than over cocktails in order to establish some sort of control over its potential for abuse. Sex education seemed the answer.

But I never dreamed it would reach the point where condoms were being handed out like Mickey Mouse balloons in a clinic meant only for high school students. We weren't even allowed to say rubbers in East Oakland, much less get them for nothing.

I realize, however, that times have changed, so in order to renew my thinking I discussed the birth-control clinic with school board members Roberta Weintraub, who was co-sponsor of the idea, and David Armor, the sole dissenting vote. Both represent the San Fernando Valley.

Armor is of the opinion, to paraphrase, that sex has gotten completely out of hand and that it is time for everyone to pull up his pants and go home. Her pants too.

He believes we have become "soft on sex" and that the school board majority, by approving a clinic, is addressing not the problem but the result of the problem. Sexual promiscuity, which Armor calls the Hollywood Morality, is the problem, pregnancy the result.

Weintraub, on the other hand, while observing in passing that Armor doesn't know what he's talking about, says she doesn't care what the response to her stand is; she knows she's right.

"People are upset about it," she said, "because they don't understand the issue. It's emotional. They're saying 'When I was in high school we didn't have . . . .' Complete in 50 words or less."

Well, when I was in high school, we didn't need clinics or special education. We knew that sex was dirty, but we knew also that it was great fun. Hardly anyone got pregnant because hardly anyone got lucky.

Weintraub says she doesn't understand why everyone is so upset at the proposal to establish a high school birth-control clinic that will hand out contraceptive devices, both oral and . . . well . . . non-oral.

I do.

Not that the clinic is a bad idea, given the circumstances of a society wallowing in self-indulgence. It's just that it introduces a new element of confusion into an arena of mixed moralities that has already left everyone a little dizzy.

I mean, wasn't it just yesterday we were arguing over whether high school kids ought to eat junk food? The dichotomy is dazzling.

We live in a world of excesses. There are too many missiles, too many lawyers, too many dopers, too much sex, too many murders, too many cars, too much pollution, too many preachers, too much protest and too many experts.

What once seemed easy now seems out of control. We can't supply answers because we're still working on the questions.

I don't know what's right. I hear much of value in what Roberta Weintraub proposes and much to heed in what David Armor warns us about.

A friend of mine, in addressing the cyclical nature of human events, used to dismiss the *deja vu* by saying, "Same old circus, different clowns."

The difference today, I suppose, is that now even the clowns seem excessive, and never as funny.

— 30 —

ETHNIC

Marching to a Mad Drummer

The letter was signed only "Frank" and was carefully printed on lined notebook paper. It said that Jews were taking over the American presidency, blacks were controlling American music and Mexicans had a stranglehold on the gross national product.

It said that Jews, blacks and "people like you" were mongrelizing the Christian white race, but that the time was coming when Jews, blacks and people like me would be adequately dealt with by, one presumes, people like him.

I think I know the man. He lives in Pacoima (which was the postmark on the envelope) and writes to me whenever there is a stirring of racism in the land.

Our one-way correspondence began a few years ago after articles exploring the size and scope of hate groups in America appeared on the front page of The Times. I wrote them.

I had spent months seeking out the sick, sad misanthropes, both Nazis and Klansmen, who marched to mad drummers in a twilight army. Frank Collin in Chicago, Matthew Koehl in Arlington, David Duke in New Orleans, Tom Metzger in San Diego. Others in New York, Portland, Stockton, San Francisco, Canoga Park.

It was before Collin led the Nazi demonstrations in Chicago. Before Metzger ran for Congress in San Diego. Before exponents of a "new Klan" hit the television talk shows.

I was moved to investigate their activities by isolated instances of cross burnings and the unsettling reappearance of swastikas. Something inside said *watch them!* so I did. I'm hearing that voice again. *Watch them.*

It isn't just the letter from the nut in Pacoima that makes me uneasy. Nor a couple of telephone calls I have received, both of them also anonymous. It's the cross burning in Kagel Canyon in 1983, the anti-Semitic literature distributed at Parkman Junior High last January, the murder of a talk show host in Denver.

It's my gut talking to me. *Something's out there.*

I asked Dave Lehrer how he felt. Lehrer is Western States

Counsel for the Anti-Defamation League of B'nai B'rith and a good source on what's happening in the hate world.

"I think it's only the hard core that's stirring," he said. "They want to show that the flag is still up. Their flag."

Widespread coverage of their activities flushes them out. The same coverage, one hopes, will ultimately flush them down, but meanwhile they survive.

"In the past few months, everyone has focused on the neo-Nazis because of incidents of violence," Lehrer said. "Oddly, a side effect of the publicity is that they grow. But it isn't a systematic growth. The numbers remain small."

They're cut from the same cloth, these people, regardless of the name they go by. The American Nazi Party, the National Socialist White People's Party, the Ku Klux Klan, the Order, the Aryan Brotherhood, Posse Comitatus.

They wear hoods and Hitler brown shirts and drift from one organization to another. They distribute pamphlets, make phone calls, meet in basements, collect guns and prepare for a racial Armageddon they are certain will come.

The controversy attending Ronald Reagan's muddled indecision on whom to honor during his upcoming trip to West Germany has got them barking and scratching again. The guy in Pacoima, stirred to fighting fury, sat right down and wrote that letter. Two others sat right down and called me.

Shadows in the dark, voices in the jungle.

This morning, as I began writing about the Nazis and the Klansmen, my intent was to mock them. God created such people especially for the satirist's table. They are buffoons, ridiculous and inadequate, seething with redirected self-hatred, evil caricatures of dark history.

I remember Frank Collin particularly, living with guards and dogs in a boarded up storefront in southwest Chicago, hiding in a room behind a bright red door. I remember him coming down the stairs toward me, a paunchy, dull-eyed man in rumpled uniform trousers and unpressed olive drab shirt. He was yawning and seemed confused.

I remember thinking, *this is the new American Hitler? This mean, tongue-tied clown who can barely articulate his own hatreds? This disheveled fool with a half-zipped fly who mumbles and scratches and proclaims himself the new messiah of a super race?*

I damn near strangled to keep from laughing.

Collin, by the way, went to prison for sexually abusing young boys. He's still on parole.

But to have dismissed his potential would have been to deny my own instincts. To treat any of them as a joke would be to ignore the admonition that history repeats itself. Madmen do come to power. Arms are easily obtained and triggers just as easily pulled.

So I share with you instead the knowledge that the Nazis and the Klansmen exist in the land, and the unsettling notion that there is a stirring among them.

I say it without mockery because even that requires hard laughter, and I can't find them very funny anymore.

They're out there somewhere, possessed by a special lunacy, hearing a distant drummer.

Watch them.

— 30 —

No Magic on the Mountain

I note with interest that Six Flags Magic Mountain, the Valencia amusement center for white people, is stopping suspected gang members at the gate in an effort to ensure the safety of non-gang members who visit the park.

Wide notice has been given to the center's policy of searching and/or refusing entry to those who might cause problems for others.

I don't mean stock swindlers or perjurious government leaders, by the way. They represent an acceptable element of American mischief-making that limits itself to lying and stealing.

We're talking here of kids who lack the guile to make money at *real* crime and who might, at any moment, turn an otherwise peaceful arena of family fun into a primitive battle zone.

No one wants to survive a bone-jarring, 3-G carnival ride only to be gunned down at the cotton candy wagon.

The idea of curtailing gang violence isn't altogether a bad one in a city where drive-by shootings have become almost as common as silicone breast implants.

But, how, I hear you ask, can a security guard at Magic Mountain be certain beyond doubt that the man he's barring at the gate is indeed a gang member?

Good question.

Unfortunately, however, no one at the park is willing to reveal his methods, so we are left, alas, to speculate on our own.

To begin with, refusing entry to those who *appear* to be gang members isn't good enough. Appearance is often deceiving.

I, for instance, could easily pass as a twisted Cuban terrorist and be refused admittance at Magic Mountain on the basis of my potential for hijacking a roller coaster and demanding that it take me to Havana.

I don't even like roller coasters.

Similarly unreliable is the method that identifies gang members by their "colors," which is to say some obvious symbol of their wicked allegiance: "Eastside Assassins" emblazoned on their scruffy jackets, for instance, with "Death to the Gringos" underneath.

122

Simple enough if we could rely on gang members to dress as they ought to, but they are an unpredictable lot and cannot be trusted to act according to their class.

Worse, *cholo chic* has become a popular style of dress among young gringos who are not members of gangs themselves, but who have taken to wearing gang colors.

Often in affluent areas, for instance, you'll find white teenagers getting out of their BMWs wearing silk sport coats with "Malibu Mafia" emblazoned on the back and "Death to Data Processors" underneath.

Denying them entry on that basis portends real trouble.

You might get by booting minorities out of an amusement park on the basis of evil intent, but you start kicking out the white bread, brother, and a lot of the magic, which is to say the gross receipts, is going to spew out of the mountain.

I'm sure all of this, however, has been taken into consideration by park security forces, and the aforementioned methods of gang identification rejected as unsuitable.

They have also undoubtedly rejected the use of dogs to sniff each suspected gang member for drugs and rubber hoses to make a kid talk when a guard knows sure as hell he's a *vato loco* in disguise.

But, if all of that is rejected, just how *do* they determine who is a gang member and who isn't? What *is* the secret method by which they are able to circumvent due process by recognizing beforehand exactly who is guilty until proven innocent?

I think they've got a Wizard on Magic Mountain.

There's someone up there with psychic powers beyond those anyone could imagine, someone that Toto would never find pumping smoke behind a concealing screen, someone real, someone grand, someone all-knowing.

Normally, the Wizard probably declines to use the powers God gave him, but he finds now he must. Gang violence has gotten out of hand. They aren't just killing their own anymore. They're killing you. They're killing me. They're killing *us*.

The Wizard is afraid.

Hell, man, we're all afraid, but history is full of the kinds of response to fear that defames human dignity and suppresses human rights.

A fear of devils, a fear of witches, a fear of communists, a fear of infidels, a fear of pagans, a fear of madness, a fear of disease, a fear of each other.

The dead have been piled like cordwood down the bloody centuries and the living encaged like animals in violent efforts to protect *us* from *them*, by whatever means.

It's time we learned. Fear isn't good enough anymore to justify actions specifically prohibited by enlightened documents. Fear, as a weapon of public order, is more terrifying in its portent than gangs.

Magic Mountain is seeking simple solutions to a difficult problem and, so doing, is failing to perceive a danger that precedence imposes. Denying the rights of one is to deny the rights of all.

Thomas Jefferson put it differently, but the truth remains as bright today as it did 200 years ago.

There is no magic in a free society, and there are sure as hell no wizards.

— 30 —

Three Jews, Two Asians and a Mexican

The Jonathan Club of Santa Monica is once more fighting back against accusations that it discriminates on the basis of race and national origin. Just recently the club proudly announced that among its members are three Jews, two Koreans and a Mexican.

Well, actually, it announced the three Jews and two Asians. However, I know for a fact that one light-colored Mexican is also among the club's estimated 3,000 members.

That brings to two-tenths of 1% the known representation of minorities in a private organization to which the state of California is willing to lease public-trust land.

All of this was revealed at a recent meeting of the California Coastal Commission, which voted to allow the Jonathan Club to expand onto state land if the club adopted a policy of nondiscrimination.

Among those at the meeting was David Lehrer who, in addition to being an attorney for the Anti-Defamation League of B'nai B'rith, is also spokesman for a coalition of Jewish, Latino, Asian, black and women's groups.

I have known David for many years and know that he will often skip breakfast and work late in order to shish-kebab a bigot. He can identify an anti-Semite in a room full of liberals while blindfolded, picking the racist out by his vibrations, like a tiger shark selects its next meal.

"All they (the club lawyers) have to do is *say* they don't discriminate and they can get the land," Lehrer told me the other day. "But they won't even do that. That's about as clear an admission of discrimination as you'll ever see."

The Jonathan people must realize that they have potentially big problems in Lehrer, so they tried to soothe him by inviting him to the Santa Monica facility. There David was told of the three Jews and two Koreans.

"They didn't mention blacks or women," he said, "which probably means they don't have any. If they had, I'm sure they'd have told me about it."

I'll never believe that the Jonathan Club doesn't discriminate on the basis of race, religion, sex or ethnicity. The most I have ever gotten out of them is that anyone can apply for membership.

That doesn't mean that anyone can actually *join,* only that they can fill out an application, a right not dissimilar to allowing blacks into an exclusive restaurant but not letting them eat. One thing at a time.

What rankles is not only that the club probably will not allow minorities to join (with the exception of those three Jews, two Asians and a Mexican) but, as far as I'm concerned, it also flaunts a discriminatory stance and blocks off the ocean at the same time.

Fifty years ago, American author and social activist Charlotte Gilman wrote, "I ran against a prejudice that quite cut off the view."

She wasn't talking about the Jonathan Club, but her observation applies. The club sits like a pimple on the nose along Pacific Coast Highway, daring anyone to challenge its existence. But most of the potential challengers are busy opposing racial segregation in South Africa. Bigotry is always easier to fight when it belongs to someone else.

The city of Santa Monica, once known as the People's Republic for its liberal attitudes, is not likely to be in the forefront of those who want to close the Jonathan Club. Just last year, in fact, the City Council signed a long-term lease with the club on land it already occupies.

The rationale among the council's liberals was that if they hadn't signed, the club would have just gone to court and won the case anyhow. It was, of course, "personally repugnant" to them, but personal repugnancy, thank God, has a way of dissipating overnight.

I imagine that the Jonathan's attorneys are discussing at this very moment methods by which they can circumvent the non-discrimination demands of the California Coastal Commission.

One way would be to welcome into their membership another Mexican, a bisexual black and a Native American midget from Arizona.

By combining two sexes in one black and claiming two minorities in one for the Native American, the Jonathan Club could then claim three Jews, two Asians, two Mexicans, one black, a woman, a gay, an Indian and one physically deprived out-of-stater.

Even that could be condensed by signing up a handicapped bisexual female black who is converted to Judaism. It would be nice if she were married to a Puerto Rican, but you can't have everything.

I have a feeling that the Jonathan Club is going to do all it can to remain exactly what it is, in which case David Lehrer's coalition ought to simply take a new approach. Not a demand to allow minorities into the club, but a demand to not let the racists out.

Then we will at least know where some of them are at all times and, given the nature of a world more aware of human rights, I doubt that anyone will miss them.

Their kind of prejudice has blocked the view of a decent world long enough.

— 30 —

A
Quiet
Triumph
of
Hate

Hate won last weekend in Westchester, a small, tense community south of Los Angeles. Tori and Robson Dufau, their lives and their children threatened by a bigot, moved from their neat stucco home on West 79th Street.

There was no fuss and there was no fanfare.

They were driven out by a barrage of racist mail that climaxed in the shooting death of a pet rabbit in their backyard.

But the rabbit wasn't the real target. They were. The reason: Tori is black, her husband white.

"I wanted to stay," she told me a few days ago. "I wanted the bigots to know they couldn't get away with what they were doing.

"But it began affecting our whole family. There was no other choice. They *did* get away with it."

The Dufaus moved into the house last October. The hate mail began a month later.

The swastika-lined literature ranted against "niggers" and railed against race-mixing. "The zoo wants you," one letter said.

The harassment hurt and angered the young couple, but it didn't terrorize them. They vowed not to move from the house they had leased with option to buy.

There was more at stake here than their own welfare. There was a principle involved.

But then their car was pelted with eggs. Notes were dropped in a front door slot during brief absences from the house. The pet rabbit was in a backyard pen when it was shot to death.

The Dufaus began to suspect that their enemy was not a remote bigot, but a neighbor. They felt watched and in immediate danger. They bought a gun.

"Neither of us could sleep," Tori said. "We were getting paranoid about who might be doing all this. We were on edge."

They called the Los Angeles Police Department, which made a public relations appearance at a block meeting but otherwise did very little.

130

Both the FBI and the regional postal inspector refused to become involved. It wasn't their department. It wasn't in their jurisdiction.

Only the Westside Fair Housing Council seemed to care or want to help. A support group was organized. The hate mail continued.

"We lost complete confidence in the police," Tori said. "Three months ago, I gave them some literature that had been hand-delivered. It had a clearly visible fingerprint on it. They said they would check it but did nothing. They haven't even called us back."

Responding to the growing fear in different ways, Tori began to gain weight, Robson to lose it.

"I think on our own we would have continued to stick it out," Tori said. "But there was our son to consider. I couldn't subject him to any more."

They have two children, both boys. The eldest son, just 5, is the one they worried about most. The death of his pet rabbit did something to him.

"I took him to a dentist one day," Tori said. "The receptionist took me aside later and said he had asked her to be his mother."

When Tori questioned the boy about it, he replied that he wanted a white mommy so that the trouble would end.

"It's gotten him confused," Tori said. "He now feels it's not OK to be black."

The final letter came two weeks ago.

It said that the continued presence of Tori and Robson Dufau was angering a growing number of those who did not want them in Westchester. It added: "If you stay, you'll pay."

"I guess that really did it for us," Tori said. "I am angered and saddened we couldn't hang on, but the danger was too great. That was the end."

I talked with Blanche Rosloff, who is executive director of the Westside Fair Housing Council.

"This kind of thing is happening more and more," she said. "Everyone says 'Blanche, this will go away,' but it won't. It's getting more personal and more threatening."

On any given day in the Westside, you could probably gather a thousand noisy marchers to parade against everything from apartheid in South Africa to hunger in Ethiopia.

But despite newspaper and television exposure of their plight, no one marched for Tori and Robson Dufau, no one yelled, no one picketed and damned few even seemed to really care.

And so it was at the end.

There were no trumpets sounded at any time by the brother-hood activists who willingly wage remote warfare against Pretoria but who wouldn't lift a picket sign to support a troubled family in Westchester.

Commitment, it seems, increases in direct proportion to the distance from a battlefield.

When the Dufaus moved, they moved without audience, though there was a form of spectral companionship in the ghost that shadowed their packing.

They gave occupancy of their old neighborhood over to an evil that lives beyond the light, that thrives in places where love dies and malice festers.

I drove by the home once occupied by the Dufaus. Shades are drawn over the windows. An air of despair and abandonment shrouds the emptiness.

There is, indeed, a haunting of hatred going on here.

Racism won when a young family was driven from a neighbor-hood in Westchester. But, by the tone of that victory, it was not only the Dufaus who suffered defeat.

We all lost.

— 30 —

Music
in
the
Night

It was one of those misty Santa Monica nights that remind me of San Francisco, when fog wets the streets and mutes the
ordinary sounds of traffic. People were walking around with their
collars turned up and even a loud laugh sounded intrusive.

Voices ought to be low when the fog rolls in.

I had just come from a performance of something called
"Tomfoolery" at the Burbage Theater in West L.A., which I thought
might make a column for me, but it didn't. I was naturally depressed.

Not that the performance was bad. In fact it was pretty good,
but I just couldn't buy all that spunk and perkiness to tunes by Tom
Lehrer, probably the best satirist in the last 50 years.

None of the ironies came through, and if you don't have irony
you don't have Lehrer.

So I was drifting around at midnight when I decided to stop for
a late one at Bob Burns', because there's nothing like hunching over
a Glenlivet on the rocks when a mist is on the ocean. It's a perfect
time for self-pity.

That's where I met Mario.

I was sitting in a corner sipping Scotch and listening to Doug
Sprague play the piano, when suddenly this fat man stood up.

Doug noticed him and said "Mario" without missing a beat and
handed him a mike, then flowed into one of the Beatles' tunes,
"Yesterday." Perfect.

Mario, who had been sitting at one end of the piano bar, began
to sing.

He was in his shirt sleeves and his shirt tail was half sticking
out, so I figured he was probably one of the patrons and not part of
the act. Also, he had tattoos on both arms.

There weren't too many people in the place because Thursday
is not one of your big drinking nights. Mario was not exactly performing to a packed house.

But that didn't seem to bother him a bit. He closed his eyes and really got into the tune, kind of swaying and moving his free hand in a wavelike motion.

I began to wonder who he was beyond being a fat guy with tattoos, because I was thinking he is not half bad. I mean, maybe he's Bruce Springsteen or Robert Goulet, neither of whom I would recognize.

I made it a point to talk to Mario after he was finished doing a duet with Doug. That's when I found out who he was. A guy with dreams on a foggy night.

His name is Mario Reyes. He is 32 years old, the son of people who own a Mexican fast-food restaurant in East L.A., and when he was a kid he used to sleep with his radio on, he loved music so much.

By the time he was 12 he had learned to play the guitar by ear and pretty soon he was organizing his own band, something called "Black Magic Express."

For years he did his damndest to make it to the big time, knocking on doors and playing the dives at $10 a shot, but it just didn't happen. As he put it that night at Bob Burns', "I never broke through."

So Mario went to work in the family restaurant.

Now a lot of guys would just let it go at that, if you know what I mean, forgetting the boyhood dance with dreams to stumble along like everybody else on the long, hard road of reality.

But not Mario.

He could still hear the song in his heart and he could still imagine himself in front of a crowd, swaying like he does, with his eyes shut, making music.

"All I need," he would tell everybody, "is a chance."

Mario is a night creature and he and his pals took to partying at the Santa Monica Pier, so it was natural that pretty soon he would discover Bob Burns', just a whisper from the ocean.

It's a decent place to drink and Doug Sprague plays the kind of music meant for night-prowlers.

"I began harmonizing with Doug kind of on my own," Mario said, "and then one night about a year ago he says, 'This is made for a duet' and shoves a mike at me.

"I start to sing, you know, and it feels good, and I've been coming in ever since."

It is not usual that a performer will willingly share the spotlight with a guy who wanders in off the street, so I asked Doug why he does it with Mario.

"I like him," Doug said. "He's different."

You know what I think it is? It's Mario's dream that comes shining through.

He wants more than anything to be making music about midnight in a place like this, and he does it for nothing just to keep the hope burning, the way a fighter stays at it even when he knows he'll never be champ.

We can all relate to a guy who won't give up, who can schlep tacos in the daytime and sing at night, because a lot of us yearn for Mario's kind of tenacity, in the dark places of the soul where our own dreams are buried.

I listened for a while longer, finished my Scotch and left, feeling oddly better about everything because the fat man was at the mike and Doug was letting him be there. That's not bad.

That's not bad at all.

— 30 —

The Class
That Money
Can Buy

It comes as no surprise that the Los Angeles City Council hates crime and poverty. However, unlike many legislative groups that spend months and perhaps years attempting to alleviate their causes, L.A. has come up with what appears to be a quick, sure-fire method of eliminating them overnight: You simply send them someplace else.

This is implicit in a neighborhood renewal plan that would force 3,000 low-income Latinos out onto the street to make way for renovation of the apartments they now occupy. This, in turn, would allow for an influx of, as proponents of the plan suggest, "a new class of tenants."

Exit crime and poverty, hello happiness.

The way it works, see, is that by upgrading 30 buildings in question, the apartment owners could then raise the rent. This would effectively block the poor from moving back in. And once you get rid of the poor, you're just naturally going to eliminate all the grubby street crime. People with money break the law on a higher, more sophisticated level.

South Africa has solved its racial problems in a similar manner by sending its blacks to the social equivalent of Someplace Else, and everyone knows how well it has worked in Johannesburg.

To thank for the L.A. proposal we have none other than Hal Bernson, God's best friend on the City Council. Hal is a former T-shirt salesman and conservative Republican who represents the Northridge area of L.A.

His prior methods of solving social problems generally follow along the lines taken by his current plan to eliminate crime and poverty.

Three years ago, responding to the complaints of business interests, Bernson declared war on street vendors and, through the judicious use of the Department of Building and Safety, chased the vendors northeast into another district.

Earlier this year, responding to the complaints of real estate in-

138

terests, he declared war on topless bars and dirty bookstores, demanding that they be driven out of his district and clustered in an industrial area someplace else.

And two weeks ago he began applying the Someplace Else Theory of social adjustment to crime and poverty.

The City Council, in a preliminary vote, approved the proposal that could soon become law, to the detriment of the poor but to the happiness of that New Class waiting just around the corner.

Fighting poverty by making money has always been the American Way. There just seems to be a little confusion about who ought to be making it, that's all.

The councilman and his backers in the Instant Redevelopment Plan deny with some heat that there is anything racist about their intentions. It is simply a coincidence that the 3,000 tenants are mostly Latino. If they were mostly black they'd get thrown out just as fast.

Bernson explained at one point that he simply wanted "good" tenants in the area. Apparently, Latinos are not good tenants, an extrapolation of the national policy that has won us so many friends south of the border.

Members of the council who voted for Bernson's Good Tenant Proposal, by the way, are now saying that they didn't realize exactly what it involved and endorsed it only as a courtesy to a colleague. One can only be grateful that good old Hal wasn't declaring war on Canada.

To someone with a city councilman's limited perceptions, the idea of what-you-don't-see-can't-hurt-you must be appealing. By shipping the poor and their taco-tinted crime wave out of Northridge, Bernson is, to the best of his intellectuality, solving the problem.

The poor Latinos may not like it, but then they aren't the ones who contribute to good old Hal's campaigns.

What struck me most as I walked through the neighborhood that Bernson wants to remake in his own image is not the condition of the apartments that so offends the councilman's sense of Anglo aesthetics, but the great presence of children in the three-block complex.

Their voices ride the wind as they play in their yards, on the sidewalks and in the alleys behind their homes—homes, incidentally, that poor people around the world would die to possess.

The message the City Council imparts to them, whether intended or not, is a message of racism written for the sake of political expediency and temporary solutions. They don't belong here, they belong in a Land of Someplace Else, out of sight and out of mind.

If good old Hal is allowed his way, that neighborhood of 30 apartment units will indeed be swept relatively clean of crime and poverty.

One can't help but wonder, though, what new dangers await as the years pass and the children grow and the angry armies of Someplace Else call us to account for the arrogance and ignorance of a man who used to sell T-shirts.

— 30 —

The

Do-Do King

I was being interviewed the other day on the telephone by a college student who said that writing a newspaper column must require a precise command of semantic skills and an ability to convey thematic messages in a quick and concise fashion.

I said, "Huh?"

"You have to say what you mean and mean what you say," she said snappily.

I said, "Oh, yeah, right."

"Deciding what subject to tackle must necessitate thought and evaluation, weighing the importance and immediacy of one issue against the other, measuring broad impact against personal preference."

"Yeah, I guess so."

"For instance, Mr. Hernandez, have you selected your column topic for Thursday?"

"The name is Martinez."

"Of course."

"You sure you've got the right person?"

"Oh yes," she said. "The assignment is to interview a minority journalist. You're a minority?"

"Sí."

"Good. Now, about your Thursday column?"

"Yeah, well, I'm writing about this guy who picks up doggie do-do."

Silence.

"I beg your pardon?"

"Sort of the Poo Poo King of San Fernando Valley. Zeke Zeleznikar."

"He picks up doggie . . . *do-do?*"

Actually, Zeke and his partner will pick up any kind of do-do, but the primary thrust of their business are the messes left by dogs. Their motto is, "We pick up where your dog leaves off."

I met with Zeke the other day in his tiny Studio City apartment, which is dominated by a 500-pound bronze mermaid lying on a table near the front door.

Zeke is an artist and used to hustle his wares out of a van on Laurel Canyon Boulevard until the cops said you can't sell naked mermaids on a public street and chased him off.

Later Zeke gave the mermaid to Santa Monica because the city seal is a mermaid, and Zeke figured he might get a little ink out of the donation, if you know what I mean.

"They loved it," Zeke said, standing in the middle of his apartment.

He was wearing an aloha shirt, jeans, cowboy boots and a dirty white smock. He looks a little like Dr. Johnny Fever on the old "WKRP in Cincinnati" television show.

"I thought the deal was closed, and then one day I got a letter saying the decision was reversed because the mermaid was 'unfit for public sighting."

"It was the breasts," Maria Maucere said. She lives with Zeke. "They didn't like the naked breasts."

Zeke sighed. "I should've put a bra on her."

Artistically, things have not gone well for Zeke. He has made only one sale in the past 18 years, a portrait for which he was paid $5.

As a musician, he hasn't fared much better.

In 1981, Zeke organized a band he called Trash, for reasons he felt were perfectly clear.

"What I did," Zeke explained, "was to pick up a bunch of drunk musicians and keep them sober long enough to make a record. We fed them and bathed them and wouldn't let them out of our sight until the job was done."

The song was called "Wrong Number," and although everyone liked it, no one bought it.

Meanwhile, he and Maria and their dog, Ziecher, had to eat. Ziecher means rabbit hunter in Croatian.

Zeke kept them going with odd jobs but wanted work of a more consistent nature that would bring in money but not take up a lot of time, thus freeing him for artistic pursuits.

That's when he discovered the do-do business.

"I was reading a magazine story about a guy in Omaha who was making a fortune picking up poo-poo," Zeke said. "So I says, why not?"

He brought in the guy across the hall, Evan Freeman, and together they organized Pooper Scooper, distributing cards and flyers throughout the Valley.

The flyer features a kind of Thurberesque dog, which, Zeke said, he drew as a self-portrait years ago. I didn't ask him to explain.

For about $40 a month, Zeke and Evan will come to your house once a week, pick up the poo-poo and take it away. Evan wears a top hat during the calls and Zeke an artist's tam. They put the do-do in bins and garbage cans.

They began their company eight weeks ago, Zeke said, and already have two houses and a 120-unit apartment complex.

"It's bound to grow," Zeke said. "There is do-do everywhere."

The idea is not to make a fortune for themselves, he added, but to be in a financial position to borrow money from a bank to make a movie.

"A movie about what?" I asked.

"About an artist trying to make money," Zeke said.

When I explained all of this to the college student who was interviewing me, she said, "That's what you write about?"

"Sure," I said. "It's what minority journalists do. The white guys downtown get the good stuff. I get the poo-poo stories."

"I don't believe you," she said.

"Trust me," I said. "I will write it for Thursday's paper and attempt to communicate the artistic significance of the do-do endeavor in terms that will convey its thematic message quickly and concisely, not to mention semantically."

"Thank you," she said coolly, "it's been a pleasure."

De nada.

HUMOR

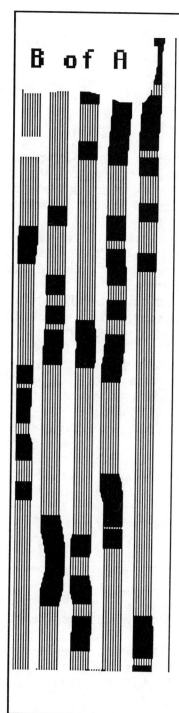

B of A

Lost
in a Memory
System

**"You deny
my existence?"**

© 1987 The Los Angeles Times

I have ordered new checks from the Bank of America. That may not seem a considerable undertaking, since anyone with a San Francisco education and a Los Angeles job can have a checking account. My problem embraces a more serious concern. I am lost in the bank's memory system.

Four times I have requested the same checks. It is not a complicated order. I ask only functional checks of a nondescript nature. I do not require designer checks, mauve-toned checks or checks that feature scenes of the sun rising over Yellowstone.

I thought I conveyed my wishes rather well in a reorder form mailed to a downtown branch of the nation's second-largest banking institution. Send me some blank checks, to hell with the frills, I will take care of the rest.

Nothing happened for several weeks, so I telephoned.

I spoke with someone named Connie, who might be going on 17. I knew I was in trouble when I explained that I wanted to place a new order for the checks and she replied, "Fabulous."

It has been my experience that anyone who *says* fabulous generally isn't.

But, God knows, Connie tried. She punched me up in her computer. I wasn't there. I would have to re-apply.

"Can you take it over the phone?" I asked amiably enough, for a person of my acrid nature.

"Fabulous," Connie said. "How do you spell your name?"

I began, "M-a-r . . . ."

"The first name."

"Al?"

*"*Yeah," she said, "that one."

"A-1," I said very slowly. I tend to slur. Sometimes Al Martinez comes out sounding like Elmer Teenez.

"Fabulous," Connie said.

I got the checks but then noticed that Connie had misspelled the name of my street. Well, it's a complicated name. Oak.

148

I telephoned again. I got Helen, an older woman assigned to fools, liars and felons attempting to defraud the bank.

"We don't show you," she said.

"You don't show me what?"

"In our computer. Are you sure you placed your order with the Bank of America?"

"I have the checks right in front of me," I said. "They have Bank of America across the top and O-k-e Street in the upper left-hand corner."

"You're *positive?*"

" I'd stake my life on it."

"Check the name again," she said.

"The hell I will!"

"Well," Helen said suspiciously, "assuming you *do* have our checks, I can only conclude you have been lost in the memory system."

"You deny my existence?"

"We don't show you," she said.

Helen suggested I appear in person at the nearest branch of the bank, which I did. I spoke with Miss Evans, a pleasant lady in her middle years.

"It's O-a-k Street and not O-k-e Street?" she asked.

"I swear to you, Miss Evans."

"Sometimes people get confused as to their street names."

"I have known individuals, Miss Evans, who do indeed become confused as to their street names. I have also known individuals who steal from churches, put ketchup on their quiche and urinate in the gutter. I am not among them. My street is named after a Live O-a-k, not a Live O-k-e or even a Live O-o-k."

"That would be a Live *Ook.*"

"Will I get new checks?"

"I'll put a rush on them." That was two months ago. No checks came. What did come, however, was a statement that revealed the Bank of America, never slow to collect, had charged me $9.20 for my reorder.

Little people with Catholic backgrounds who have been raised to respect authority have soaring faith in the ultimate veracity of their institutions. It has something to do with papal subservience. So I telephoned the Bank of America again.

I swear to you the young man who handled what has now become known as My Case said, "I don't show you."

I hardly ever cry. I rage and bellow and curse the day your

mother slept with your father or perhaps your uncle, but breaking into tears is not my style.

"Gregg," I said to him, my voice choking slightly, "help me. I am going down for the third time. My fingers are slipping off the edge. My plane is out of fuel at 44,000 feet. Give me your hand, Gregg. *For God's sake, boy, reach out!"*

"Oh," he replied pleasantly, "here you are!"

He did not actually find my order in his computer. He found the $9.20 the bank had charged for the order and reasoned that, ergo, I must have placed an order in the first place. Gregg vowed I would receive the right checks within a week.

That was six weeks ago. They have not come. I am using checks that say I live on Oke Street and, when clerks ask if that is my correct address, I lie and say yes. It is conceivable that I may go to federal prison for lying to a sales clerk while engaged in a purchase.

So be it. I do not have the strength to telephone the Bank of America again. I am even afraid now that they *will* send checks. Sure as hell they will bear the name Elmer Teenez.

— 30 —

2 + 2 = 4

4 + 4 = 8

8 + 8 =

15?

18?

14?

Next Time, Shake the Cable First

I was driving along the freeway in my faithful 280Z on a night as warm and sweet as honey in tea when it occurred to me that, all things considered, I was a pretty lucky man. I was in reasonably good health, my children were heterosexual, my column had cleared the censors and the Southern California IRS audit center had just burned down.

It was altogether a terrific evening, and I whistled a zany little tune as I enjoyed a rare moment of well-being. Then my lights went out.

I am not speaking metaphorically here. My headlights blinked to black, along with my dash lights, my turn lights and all the other lights that adorn my car. And then my engine failed.

Only those who have endured the horror can understand what it is like breaking down on a freeway.

There is never a time when traffic is light on what is known locally as the Death Strip. Try it at 4 a.m. on the Sunday following the end of the world and you will find the freeway almost as busy on Doomsday as it is during the commute hours.

I don't know why everyone is adrift in the middle of the night. They are out dealing coke or buying pizza or looking for the Swami Saraswati, who is said to be driving north toward San Francisco.

What I do know is that I was in the middle of them, lightless and powerless, as the inertia of my forward thrust faded and my speed began to drop.

I kept thinking it would be a lousy way to die and wishing I had written something more poetic as my last column and wondering how my patient wife would be able to manage our stupid dog without me.

A suburban newspaper columnist was smashed to death last night on the Ventura Freeway when his car failed in the fast lane and he was struck several times by coke-dealers, pizza-buyers and those seeking the Swami Saraswati. He is survived by his patient wife and his stupid dog. His last column could have been better.

Then the lights went on again.

I could accept this as divine intervention and fall to my knees in prayer on the shoulder of the road or I could get the hell off the freeway and find a gas station. Prudence suggested the latter.

I found a station operated by someone who could speak English and who could understand something other than how to turn on a gas pump. The attendant listened as I explained in some detail everything I knew about my problem, after which he scratched his genitals, spit on the ground, got in the car and, as they say, cranked 'er up.

"Starts good," he said, getting out again.

"Starting good," I explained, "is not the problem."

I went over it all again, and he said, "You been foolin' with the light switch?"

"Why would I be foolin' with the light switch?"

He shrugged and spit again. "Some people do."

Clearly the man was not up to dealing with power shortages in a clean, well-kept 280Z, so I moved down the street to another station, the honey-sweet night rapidly taking on the acrid nature of hemlock and hard liquor.

"Tell you what, Elmer," the mechanic said, "you come back in coupla hours and I'll have it fixed."

Under stress, I had slurred my name again and he thought it was Elmer Teenez.

"Coupla *hours?*" I whined.

He nodded.

"What do I do for a coupla hours?"

The car had been running and it suddenly stopped. Then, on its own, it started again.

"Well," I said, "I'll think of something."

I wandered into a cowboy bar that smelled of beer and urine but shortly wandered out again. It wasn't the beer and urine or even the large drunken cowboys that caused me to leave, but I'll be damned if I'll drink in a place that only plays "Okie from Muskogee" on the jukebox.

I drifted through the darkness into a Denny's, which you otherwise could not force me into at the point of a spear tipped in sputum, but there was no place else to go.

"Coffee," I said.

"That's *all?*" the waitress demanded.

Her tone was hostile. My mood was sour.

"No," I said, "as a matter of fact, I would like some coffee, some *cachat d'Entrechaux* cheese, a bowl of *potage a la tortue* and a whole suckling pig."

The manager was listening and he said, "We don't want trouble, pal."

I left, coffeeless. Back at the service station, the attendant said, "Good news, Elmer."

"You fixed it?"

"Didn't have to. Ain't broken."

"But it *is!*" I insisted.

I went over the problem again. A woman waiting nearby overheard.

"Shake the battery cable," she said.

I did. The car started. The cable began to smoke.

"It's a short," she said. "Next time shake the cable first."

Then she left. Who was that masked woman?

I had the cable replaced for $12 and the car has operated efficiently ever since. Furthermore, I continue in reasonably good health, my columns still clear the censors and my children remain, to the best of my knowledge, firmly heterosexual.

— 30 —

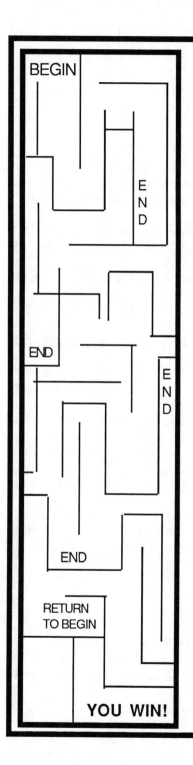

**Somewhere
Over
the Rainbow**

© 1987 The Los Angeles Times

I am sitting here staring into space, exhausted by the effort it has taken to communicate a simple request to the people at Cigna Health Plan, an organization that purports to be interested in my general welfare.

It was an uncomplicated message delivered in a calm, clear voice with absolutely no trace of an accent. To the best of my knowledge, I pronounced all of the words correctly.

But Cigna was never able to grasp even the *spirit* of my request, and that inability has driven me to the brink of madness.

It began with a telephone call to the medical facility nearest me. A woman answered.

I said, "Hello. My name is Al Martinez. I am a member of Cigna.

"Yesterday I received in the mail a booklet from Cigna outlining a program concerning use of private physicians. I lost the booklet and would like to get another. Can you help me?"

She said, *"What?"* in the kind of arrogant, incredulous tone that suggested I might have asked if she'd ever had sex with a duck.

It is a response I especially dislike, and at one stage of my life I would have eaten my way through the telephone to her head. I have learned, however, to deal with limited perception, so I simply repeated the message.

"Hello. My name is Al Martinez. I am a member of Cigna.

"Yesterday I received in the mail a booklet from Cigna outlining a program concerning use of private physicians. I lost the booklet and would like to get another. Can you help?"

"What is it you want?" she said.

I couldn't believe it.

"What part is it that baffles you?"

"You want some kind of booklet?"

"Some kind of booklet will do," I said.

"You'll have to call our North Hollywood office," she said.

Fair enough. I decided this time, however, to couch the request on a more primitive level:

"Hi," I said, "name's Al and I'm with you guys. Cigna shot me a booklet in the mail and I went and lost the little sucker. It's about, you know, private doctors an' stuff. Can you help me out, honey?"

She said, "Who is it you want?"

I said, "Hello. My name is Al Martinez. I am a member of Cigna . . . ."

"Wait a minute," she said, "I'll connect you with customer relations."

Someone named John took the call.

"John," I said, "you may be my last chance. My name is Al Martinez. I am a member of Cigna."

I paused to let that sink in.

John said, "Yes?"

"Yesterday I received in the mail a booklet from Cigna outlining a program concerning use of private physicians. I lost the booklet and would like to get another. Can you help me?"

Silence. Then John said, "I'm sorry, go ahead."

"Go ahead?"

"I had to leave the line for a moment."

"Damn, John, I'm not going over the whole thing again!"

"OK," he said, "do this. Call our corporate office. It's a toll-free number. They can help you."

I called the corporate office. My hand was beginning to tremble.

"Hello. My name is Al Martinez . . . ."

"Hold please," the operator said.

A moment later another voice said, "How can I help you?"

I had no idea who the operator had connected me to. I had only given her my name. Was there a department that dealt specifically with people named Al Martinez?

"Hello," I said, "my name is Al Martinez . . . ."

I explained everything, adding touches heretofore omitted, repeating whole phrases, dramatizing for emphasis, utilizing instincts honed over a lifetime of refining the simple, declarative sentence.

She said, "I don't know what you're talking about."

My jaw began to tighten.

I said, "Is there anyone there on any level who has absolutely any knowledge, however slim, of booklets Cigna might have either published or distributed? Take your time. Think about it."

"Just a minute," she said.

Music came on. I believe it was "Somewhere Over the Rainbow."

I waited. And waited. And waited.

It was obvious that my question would never be answered by Cigna. I hung up. Then I was taken with a great notion. Health plans are handled here at God's Chosen Newspaper by the Employee Benefits Department. *They* would know.

"Hey," I said to the woman who answered, "this is Al Martinez. Cigna sent me some stuff in the mail and I lost it and am trying to get a copy. How do I go about it?"

She said, "You want to talk to Al Martinez?"

It was unreal.

"I *am* Al Martinez!" I said.

"Who?"

"My God, woman, help me!"

She said, "One moment, please."

She put me on hold. And disappeared.

I called the extension again and a recorded voice said no one was there but I could leave a message. I did. That was weeks ago. No one ever returned the call.

I feel it is not my destiny to know whether I can get a copy of a booklet distributed by Cigna, but if anyone should ever call me back, I'm ready:

Hello. My name is Al Martinez. I am a member of Cigna. Back in 1987 I received in the mail . . . .

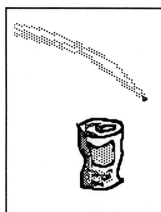

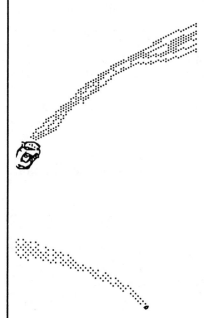

It's Just
Over the
Beer Can

A hippie got out of
the truck. He had
neither shaved,
combed his hair nor
bathed for three
years, eight months
and 22 days.

I was awakened at 3 a.m. by my wife shaking me and whispering, "It's time."

I do not believe there are two more terrifying words in the English language, relating as they often do to the imminent birth of a human child and the necessity of the male progenitor to rush his mate to a proper place of delivery.

My wife, of course, knows that and uses it as a kind of psychological cattle prod when I am likely to be slow getting up. It worked.

"Time!" I shouted, bolting upright, tending in stress to repeat the last word of every sentence.

I swung my legs out of the blankets before she could say another word and leaped nimbly onto the floor. Well, actually, I leaped nimbly onto the dog, who sleeps by the bed.

Hoover, who is not very smart and not very brave, yowled in fear and bolted toward the door, though, sad to say, the door was closed, and Hoover bounced off.

"For God's sake," my wife said, "hold it, will you? Everybody stay calm. We're just going to see Halley's Comet!"

Oh, *that.*

I had forgotten the pledge, offered in a moment of foolish acquiescence, to rise early and view the comet before it went shooting off into the starry corners of space.

"Coffee," I said weakly.

She patted my shoulder. "You just sit right there, Elmer, and I'll bring you a caffeine transfusion."

Elmer, as I have mentioned before, relates to a tendency to slur my name. People think I am saying Elmer Teenez. My whole family often calls me Elmer, although sometimes they call me Wally. I had to meet a man once named Wally and, since I forget names, I kept repeating it in my head. *Wally, Wally, Wally* . . . .

When we met, I was thinking *he's Wally and I'm Al* but I panicked and said, "Hi, I'm Wally!" "Hey," he said, "my name's Wally too!" Small world.

"Here's a place," my wife said.

I pulled the car off the road. We were on Saddle Peak Drive in the Santa Monica Mountains. The view was southeast out of Malibu Canyon.

We had built a star tracer out of a wire coat hanger and plastic wrap and knew exactly where to look. My wife spotted the comet after a few moments.

"There it is!" she said. The wonders of nature fire her imagination. Awe crept into her voice. She was out there on the star trails, lost in the cosmic silence.

The comet was a faint blur above the horizon. I studied it through binoculars until a battered old pickup parked behind us.

A hippie got out of the truck. He had neither shaved, combed his hair nor bathed for three years, eight months and 22 days. I once lived in Berkeley and am familiar with the Filthy Hippie Factor.

He also wore a dirty T-shirt, dirty jeans and dirty feet, which is to say he was shoeless. He carried a can of dirty Budweiser beer.

"You're looking the wrong way," he said.

"No I'm not," Joanne said.

She is not easily intimidated. I, on the other hand, am wary of strangers who appear on a mountainside before dawn drinking beer.

I read in Reader's Digest once that people who do not bathe are more inclined toward random violence than those who are well-scrubbed.

"Oh," I said pleasantly to the filthy hippie, "where would you say the comet is?"

I edged slightly upwind.

"That way." He pointed due west with his Budweiser. "You can make a fist and look just above it."

"Sure," Joanne said, "right over the top of your beer can."

I am not what you would call a cowardly person, but on the other hand I am not what you would call a crazy person. The filthy hippie was probably 6-2 and not in bad shape for someone who lived on beer and garbage. Furthermore, he was armed with a can.

I, on the other hand, am small and, well, delicate. I used to hear my mother whisper to friends in a tone of dismay, "He has fragile bones and throws up easily."

"Maybe," I suggested cheerfully, "there are two comets!"

They both turned to look at me. My wife smiled wryly. The filthy hippie, however, was considering the possibility.

"My old man told me once there might be two," he finally said.

I could visualize the filthy hippie and his filthy daddy, each carrying a dirty can of Bud, standing on a pre-dawn mountaintop somewhere, searching the western sky.

"Hold the bottom of your beer can on the horizon," the filthy father is saying, "and just above it you'll see one comet, maybe two or three. Now rustle me up another one them garbage-meat sandwiches, boy."

My wife ignored him and watched the fading image of Halley's Comet until the first faint light of morning trimmed the horizon in gold.

The filthy hippie continued to stare due west, weaving slightly in a tight, clockwise circle, muttering.

He was still standing there when we left, but we had to make a U-turn at the top of the road and come back in the same direction, by which time he had turned to face southeast and was holding his beer can up, peering over the top.

It was a compromise.

— 30 —

"When a satirist
feeds on human
folly," I said, "he
often dines alone."

"Oh, brother," she
said.

I talk that way
when I've been
drinking.

Life
of
the Party

There is no question in my mind that at least 82% of Los Angeles is composed of people who consider themselves either actors or writers.

This does not mean they are actually working full time at it, only that they have "puttered" at performing, as one person told me, or "dabbled" in writing, as another said.

It may be all right to putter at performing, which is what I suspect most of them do anyhow, but it isn't smart to dabble in writing. I tried it once and an editor dabbled back. The result was chaos. I haven't dabbled since.

The 82% figure popped into my head near the end of a dinner party.

"Do you realize how many people here claim to be actors or writers?" I whispered to my wife.

"They're nice folks," she said, "leave them alone."

"I'm not about to physically assault them," I said, "though God knows we would all benefit from the exercise and excitement."

"But you *are* thinking of writing a column about them, right?"

"The thought did cross my mind."

"They'll never invite you back."

"When a satirist feeds on human folly," I said, "he often dines alone."

"Oh, brother," she said.

I talk that way when I've been drinking. Sometimes I raise one finger in Shakespearean style. Unfortunately, however, I also have a tendency to stare myopically, and it appears as though I am addressing the nose of the person I'm speaking to.

One couple we met at the party were typical of the others. Roger and Jeannie are not their real names, but should be. She would spell it Gini and he would precede his first name with an initial. J. Roger Pomeroy, Author.

We were thrust together in the grand caprice of party mingling and, for lack of anything better to say, J. Roger asked, "What do you do?"

"I'm a male prostitute," I said.

"He's a writer," my wife added pleasantly.

J. Roger studied me from under an arched eyebrow. He was bearded and wore a rumpled corduroy jacket and wool slacks. That's the way a *real* writer dresses. I, on the other hand, was thrown together in the styleless manner of a shoe clerk.

"Roger is a writer too!" Gini chirped. "I'm an actress!"

She cocked her head when she talked. I cocked my head back. "Oh?" I said.

I felt as though the room were tilted.

In addition to cocking her head, Gini also thrust her breasts forward. They were pointed and angled upward, constituting a kind of screen resume.

All of Gini appeared delicately balanced. I had the feeling that if she uncocked her head before she unthrust her bosom, she'd fall to the floor.

"I'll bet," I said to J. Roger, "you have a full-time job somewhere and are working on a screenplay in your spare time and once had a story idea optioned for $500 but nothing came of it."

"Boy," Gini chirped, "are you good!"

J. Roger scowled.

"And you, Gini Bosoms," I said, "have probably done some soft porn for companies that knock 'em out in a week, and someday you want to play Grushenka, the tragic courtesan, in 'The Brothers Karamazov.' "

"The brothers who?" Gini said, puzzled.

The cock of her head increased, but thank God so did the thrust of her breasts, thus avoiding the dangerous overtilt-thrust factor that so often results in serious injury.

"Tell you what," my wife said, taking my arm, "why don't we mingle over this way, Martinez, or even that way."

"I'd like to know what *he* has written," J. Roger said to her.

"He has a right to know," I agreed.

My wife shrugged and said to J. Roger, "You're on your own."

J. Roger observed me. He put one hand in a pocket of his corduroy jacket. His left eyebrow arched. He was moving in for the kill.

"You know," I said before he could speak, "I've always wanted to be able to arch an eyebrow. Were you born that way or did you study arching somewhere?"

"What have you written?" he demanded loudly.

I could feel the hot wind of his question rush past my ear. Silence. The eyebrow remained arched. Gini remained tilted. My wife shook her head.

"This really feels good," I said. "A silence laced with emotional tension. You don't find that too much anymore."

"What have you written?" J. Roger Pomeroy asked again.

My wife intervened. "He wrote 'Death of a Salesman,' 'A Midsummer Night's Dream,' 'E.T.' and 'Origin of the Species.' "

"God," Gini said, "that's really good."

J. Roger said nothing. He grabbed Gini's arm and jerked her away, causing an abrupt and uncoordinated torso realignment that often creates an effect not unlike sudden decompression in the punctured cabin of an orbiting spacecraft.

I prayed Gini would not explode.

"Did I really write 'Death of a Salesman'?" I asked my wife. "I hope so."

"Come on, Martinez," she said, leading me out, "I'll buy you a quiet cognac. When a satirist's wife joins in the feast on human folly, at least they can have a drink together later."

What a woman.

— 30 —

R

Two
Old Ladies
in Fedco

" . . . Harold used
to want me to meet
him for lunch. The
most I did was meet
him for a drink."

"Lunch is
too important."

"My exact thought."

I like old ladies. I like them though they are often miserable human beings who crowd in front of others at the supermarket and occasionally tell someone to get the hell out of their way.

Sometimes it is difficult to like them, most notably when they are behind the wheel of a car bearing down on you and not about to slow, swerve or otherwise avoid smashing you against the side of a building.

But they are still a breed apart, brightened by years of wear to a gleaming patina of natural tones, as tart and snappy as an early winter.

I mention this by way of leading into a conversation overheard recently at a Fedco department store in the San Fernando Valley.

Two old ladies, probably in their 80s, were standing near women's wear discussing poor Harold.

I was in the area not because I have taken to hanging around the changing rooms but because I spend a good portion of my life waiting. I am an expert at it. Sometimes, just to pass the time, I wait even though there is no one special to wait for.

On this particular day, Fedco, which is one of those busy, often chaotic, warehouse-type department stores, was especially jammed. It was like the basement of Filene's in Boston, which represents the epitome of urban retail warfare.

Pushing and shoving was invented in the basement of Filene's but it was refined to an art form in Southern California.

The only place I could find to wait in safety at Fedco was near blouses and pants, which is where the aforementioned old ladies were conversing. What drew my attention to them was the opening moment of their discussion:

"I just saw Harold. He's really depressed."

"That's a bad sign."

"But for 13 years, he's had no feet. What do you expect?"

"Oh my God."

I had fallen into my normal Waiting Mode, eyes glazed over

168

and half-hypnotized by the blur of activity around me when that exchange floated across. Naturally I listened.

"You didn't know he had no feet?"

"I don't think I ever saw him out of a sickbed."

"He has the arthritis, too."

"He seemed so cheerful."

"You can touch his skin and hear his bones crackle."

"That's a bad sign."

The old lady who was bearing the bad news about Harold's unfortunate condition wore a blond bouffant wig and oversized Gloria Steinem glasses. Her information was delivered in the same lighthearted manner my mother often employed when passing on news of her own illnesses which, though frequently exaggerated, were always in abundance.

I remember mom telephoned me once after having learned she had high blood pressure and announced in a voice filled with good cheer, "Well, I'm going to die!" It was nonsense, of course, but it achieved the shock value she was seeking.

The woman in Fedco who was the recipient of the news concerning Harold and who knew a bad sign when she heard one was one of those sprightly, eager old ladies who can never hear enough about someone else's misery. Harold's condition was a bonanza.

"And the stroke. You heard about that? He has no speech now."

"Dear God."

"What could he say anyhow?"

I was beginning to get a fairly good picture of Harold by this time and his condition, as sobering as it seemed, was compelling. The man was falling apart before our very eyes. Not only that, but:

"How is Evie taking this?"

"I think she's stepping out on him."

"That's a bad sign. I'll bet she's seeing poor Harold's brother."

"No, some other bum."

"Harold was no saint. When my poor Gerald was alive, God rest his soul, Harold used to want me to meet him for lunch. The most I did was meet him for a drink."

"Lunch is too important."

"My exact thought."

At this point, they both broke into laughter. The idea of preferring lunch to Harold was too funny to ignore. But very quickly the thought of him lying there listening to his bones crackle while Evie did the town overtook them once more.

"Poor Harold. It would be a blessing if he died."

"But he won't. Mark my word. My Gerald would have hated dying like that."

"When Harold could still talk, he told me he was anxious to pass beyond. He felt God would give him back his feet. How Harold missed them. Now, I guess, it doesn't matter."

"You don't think about your feet when you still have them."

"Isn't that true? We should learn to appreciate the parts of our body. It's a bad sign when we take them for granted."

"I've got to go. There's my no-good son-in-law. I'll see you at bingo?"

"I'll be there. When you visit Harold again, tell him I'm praying for him."

"I won't be seeing him too often. He doesn't have bladder control anymore."

"It's a blessing he doesn't have to leave the house."

"God plans it so well."

"Amen."

The person I was waiting for appeared.

"I almost forgot you," she said.

That's a bad sign.

— 30 —

Dining
With
Hoover

If I can make it
through the summer,
I can make it to
Christmas.

But is life
worth living
on tofuburgers?

I was eating a healthy breakfast the other morning when, after the third tasteless bite, I put my fork down in disgust and said, "I'm just not going to do it anymore."

"Good for you, dear," my wife said, getting ready for work.

"You don't even know what I'm not going to do."

"No," she said, "but I'm sure you'll be saner and happier for not doing it."

"Suppose I stop showering and brushing my teeth?"

She smiled sweetly. "You and the dog will be very happy sleeping together."

She was out the door before I could reply.

I looked at Hoover, who was lying on his blanket in a corner, staring at me. His eyes were filled with anxiety.

"Don't worry," I said, "we're not sleeping together." He seemed relieved.

Then I compared the unattractive food on my plate to the rich gravied kibbles on his plate.

"But," I added, "we may be eating together."

I'm tired of good health and substitute foods. Before me at that moment was a breakfast composed of semi-eggs and a tofu meat patty.

My coffee was decaf, my sugar was an artificial sweetener, the cream in my coffee was soy milk and the seasoning before me was sodium-free. Nothing was what it seemed.

I have been on this kind of diet for two years. The sins of the past caught up with me in 1986. Life was no longer a cabaret, old chum.

For a while, I belonged to the Pritikin Health Center, but surviving on wheat toast and sesame spread was not my cup of herbal tea.

Also, I was not crazy about treadmilling, which is a major Pritikin activity. I recall looking down rows of overweight people walking in place like fat chipmunks and thinking that hell must be composed of just such an eternal pastime.

172

In fact, there was very little about Pritikin I *did* like, including most of the trainers. One was a chirpy, bouncy woman in her mid-20s composed of muscle and bone and 0.00 milligrams of fat. Her favorite phrase was, "We are what we eat!"

I think a lack of protein had affected her ability to concentrate. She had an empty look in her eyes and often gazed off to an astral world of good health that others couldn't see. Nancy Fitness with a Shirley MacLaine vision.

I was standing in my underwear one day while she calibrated the fat on my body. There was nothing sexual about it. Fitness nuts are too involved with the Yoga of Inner Light to think about pawing and grappling.

Nancy Fitness was measuring my stomach.

"We're going to have to work on that," she said with a Great Big Tofu Smile.

She was talking about my excessive fat.

"OK," I said, "I'll work on the stomach, what part do you want?"

She stared at me quizzically for a moment, then blinked and bounced like Tigger onto a plane of organized aerobics and holistic foods, never to be seen again.

However, I continue on a modified health regimen to this day due primarily to the efforts of my wife and son to keep me alive for at least one more summer. If I can make it through the summer, I can make it to Christmas.

But is life worth living on tofu burgers?

For those who have not tried one, eating a burger with a soy bean base is like eating finely ground cardboard. I don't care that it's a natural substance, and I don't care if it's low in fat and high in carbohydrates, I say it's cardboard, and I say to hell with it.

Ditto ersatz cheese.

I wandered through a couple of health food stores yesterday. Their customers were gaunt young men with beards and painfully skinny women clinging like pit bulls to their fading 30s.

It was in a place called Mrs. Gooch's that I discovered calcium caseinate cheese.

Calcium caseinate, according to a brochure, is pure milk protein with the lactose removed. I'm not sure what lactose is, but I guess I can do without it.

The brochure points out that "Calcium Caseinate is added as a binder to hold the product together and to give it cheese characteristics . . . melting, slicing and shredding."

But am I ready for something with "cheese characteristics"?

A woman at the cheese rack said, "It doesn't have cholesterol."

There is a kind of camaraderie at health food stores. We share the secrets of high fiber foods and organic vegetables.

"That's good," I said.

"Forty-eight million Americans suffer from heart disease," she said. "Cholesterol is partly to blame."

She was holding a container of carob soy milk. Her head bobbed back and forth as she spoke, like a character in a Mickey Mouse cartoon. I realized suddenly she reminded me of Nancy Fitness.

"Twenty-five million Americans suffer from some form of mental disease," I said. "Talking to strangers is a symptom."

I bought the fake cheese and took it home. It was lousy. So I poured a martini instead.

The martini was low in fiber and high in vodka. It was delicious.

Merry Christmas, in case I'm not around.

— 30 —

90

89

1988

1987

1986

1985

1984

1983

1982

1981

1980

1

9

7

5

1

9

7

0

1

9

6

5

Memories
of Things
Gone By

I think maybe
it's because spring
is here and the sun
warms that place in
the heart that longs
for distant shores
and half-forgotten
songs . . . .

I had a terrific idea for a column 2 1/2 minutes ago, but I can't remember what it was. I went to reach for a piece of paper and a pen to write it down, but by the time I found a pen, which was in my hand, the terrific idea was gone. I had even forgotten the pen was in my hand.

This is not a new occurrence for those who might be wondering if I am at long last losing my grip. I've been this way for a long time.

When I leave for work in the morning, my wife kisses me goodby and says, "Your name is Al Martinez and you write for the L.A. Times." Sometimes, when she's angry at me, she says, "Your name is Ramon Valdez and you live in Tijuana." But I always know where I live and I come home anyhow.

When Morris Udall was running for President in 1976, his press secretary used to hand him a piece of paper every morning that said, "Your name is Mo Udall and you hate crime and poverty." He didn't become President, but he never forgot his name.

My worst time is when I arrive at the office and am expected to say "hello, Randy" and "good morning, Meegan" to those around me. That would work all right if they were all named Randy and Meegan, but, alas, that isn't the case. The fact is, I don't know who they are.

I used to get around my inability to remember names by calling the men "keed," as in "What's doing, keed?" and the women "babe," as in "Nice to see ya, babe."

But that gets a little complicated when you are introducing two people and you can't remember *either* name. "Hey, keed, meet babe" won't wash, especially if keed is someone whose name you are expected to remember, such as your father or your editor.

It would be nice if they all wore name tags, but I guess that's too much to expect.

Sports writers are the worst because it seems somehow they don't actually *need* names and therefore there is no compelling rea-

176

son to remember them. And now we have the additional problem of women sports writers who not only don't need names but who resent gender slang.

They have it in their heads that a word like babe somehow classifies them as sex objects and implies they are inferior. That's nonsense. Sex objects are not inferior. The ability to please and satisfy a man is considerably more important than tracking the earned-run average of a high school pitcher.

God didn't give women cute behinds to plunk them on locker room benches.

I'm sure that an inability to remember is somehow linked to computers. Placing more demand on those compartments of our brains that store logic requires increased lubrication to facilitate higher speeds, which in turn drains us of our precious cranial fluids and makes us forget easier.

In the days when typewriters were used to write columns, all I had to worry about was how to change the ribbon and set the margins. Not so with computers. They summon us to far greater feats of memory than ribbons and margins.

This morning, for instance, I was gazing into space trying to remember what it was I had rushed into the room to write when I suddenly noticed an italicized line atop the screen of my word processor that said: *Esc:Menu Push ParA+Sp-95% Free. 10% Thru. Edit "C:/TIMES/almtz.nes"*

Despite my imperfect memory, I know I didn't write *Esc:Menu Push ParA+Sp-etc.* because I don't write things like that. Simply *seeing* it there washed me with the same emotional confusion televangelist Jimmy Swaggart must have felt when the Lord ordered him to go forth and find a hooker.

But I realized after a moment that the line was part of the new word-processing program designed to improve the linkage between my home computer and the Sacred Computer somewhere in a candle-lit basement at Times Mirror Square.

I would therefore accept without question that *Esc:Menu Push ParA+Sp-* was now a part of my life. It's like when I was Catholic and the services were in Latin. I didn't know what they were saying, but I knew if I didn't listen I'd end up in hell.

My point is this:

Well, actually, I don't remember what my point was. I do know, however, that the necessity to remember computer commands like *Ctrl-PrtSc* and *Copy A:*.*B:/V* and a couple of hundred others is detracting from my already scant ability to recall just exactly who in the hell you are and why I started all this to begin with.

I think maybe it's because spring is here and the sun warms that place in the heart that longs for distant shores and half-forgotten songs; where a man can lie on a hilltop and gaze at a pale blue sky and deliberately forget that *Esc:Menu Push ParA+SP-* ever existed. I'm going to find that hilltop. I'll drift through the golden afternoon like a butterfly in the garden, wander among the flashing wildflowers of the emerald canyons and finally end up at home in Tijuana with Mrs. Valdez.

Then I'll have a little martini to celebrate the birth of another spring and wonder vaguely, keed, what it was I was going to write about in the first place.

— 30 —

Savoring the Tasty Fish Split

The fish split is
a banana split in
which the banana
is replaced with a
whole cooked fish
lying between
mounds of ice cream.

I have been on a diet most of my adult life due to genetic traits inherited from my parents that left me with short legs and a pot belly.

There was nothing I could do about the short legs back then, although I read recently in the National Enquirer that scientists added a foot of height to a dwarf by stretching him.

The process, according to the Enquirer, wasn't as simple as "You take one end and I'll take the other, and we'll pull." *Au contraire.*

They deliberately broke the dwarf's legs, opened a gap between the bones and let the natural healing process add height.

It is a painful and complicated operation and should not be tried at home on your little friends.

The dwarf in the before-and-after photographs, by the way, ended up not only a foot taller but better dressed.

Even if the story is true I'm probably too brittle to be stretched at my age and do not savor the notion of having my legs broken. I have ambled along on short legs this long and will make it the rest of the way without additional height.

Always, however, I have felt there was something I *could* do about my tendency toward obesity, especially as I began to drift toward the cruel middle years.

I was motivated by a vision of myself as one of those old men you see shuffling around town with a pot belly and skinny legs, wearing red checkered shorts with an unzippered fly.

I tried every diet that came along with varying degrees of success from Scarsdale to Pritikin, losing and gaining an accumulative total of about 600 pounds in the past 10 years. None of them worked over the long haul.

But at last I have found a diet that seems to suit my purpose and I want to share that with you today. Ladies and gentlemen, boys and girls, the Burbank Diet.

That is not only the name of the diet but the title of a book by

Lola Peters who created the diet in the spirit of Burbank after moving here from Bub's Crossing, Utah, wherever that is.

I was attracted to the book not only by its title and by a desperate need for a column but also by the cover picture of something the author calls a "fish split."

The fish split is a banana split in which the banana is replaced with a whole cooked fish lying between mounds of ice cream. The fish has a cherry in its mouth and whipped cream along its unscaled back.

It was such an abominable collation that I couldn't wait to read the book, which belonged to our reporter in Burbank. When I asked if I could borrow it he said, "You can *have* the damned thing."

I learned from reading "Burbank Diet" that the fish split is symbolic of its basic strategy, which Lola Peters calls "noxious combining."

The idea is to make food so unpalatable that even the crudest of individuals will not want to eat it. There are some things that even catsup won't save.

In addition to the fish split, Peters offers a variety of other possible combinations that are equally offensive. Under a category of "Down Home Noxious," for instance, she includes strawberries and cream combined with prairie oysters, and under "Gourmet Noxious," chocolate mousse and headcheese.

The "hearty-man Jello platter," pictured on Page 26, features such a vile compost of foods that I will spare you a precise description, except to ask that you imagine yourself eating a live monkey smothered in peanut butter.

An equally significant section of the book quite properly suggests that no diet is effective without exercise. True to the nature of the Burbank Diet, Peters offers some untypical methods by which one might exert one's self in the name of good health.

This ranges from the calories burned in a family feud (138 for jumping up and down, 249 for faking a heart attack) to a less strenuous form of "air walking" which, as the author points out, builds delusions of grandeur even as it sheds pounds.

My favorite is called "Putting on the Dog." It goes as follows: "1. Muzzle dog. 2. Heft dog lightly in the air. 3. Settle dog around your shoulders like a shawl. 4. Walk 20 paces with dog draped around shoulders so that front legs hang straight down."

The amount of calories burned range from 12 for using a Pekingese to 227 for a Saint Bernard.

Finally, the author suggests sex as a means of weight control, to wit: "Sex is fun, sex is fulfilling and best of all, sex is nonfattening. The Burbank Diet endorses sex and plenty of it, especially at mealtimes."

There is no *specific* benefit mentioned, but I recall reading in Life magazine several years ago that the normal sex act burns 150 calories, give or take one's general interpretation of normal.

If, however, you hold sex on a more spiritual plane and reject its application as a function of dieting, and if personal ethics forbid tossing dogs around, just go for the fish split on a regular basis and you will no doubt be down to skin and bones in no time.

And meanwhile, of course, *bon appetit.*

— 30 —

Keeping Busy on a Wednesday

For most normal people, having sex is simply not the same as, say, having your dog groomed unless, of course, you've got something going with the dog groomer.

I have received several copies of the August issue of New Woman magazine, a periodical that purports to represent the interests of liberated females in a male-dominated society.

They were sent to me by feminists in order to call my attention to a column that offers "a thump on the head" to those making sexist remarks, among whom, I am pleased to report, my name is listed.

The reason I am pleased is that I am quoted alongside one of my favorite authors, Kurt Vonnegut Jr., who also won a thump on the head by writing, "Educating a woman is like pouring honey over a fine Swiss watch. It stops working."

No need to repeat *my* remark since I have already caught hell for it many times over and am satisfied to know that someone was paid $10 by the magazine for having sent it in. That is atonement enough.

I had not intended to read anything else in New Woman for the same reason I do not read anything in Architectural Digest or Fish & Game. They do not encompass my interests.

My attention, however, was captured by a large-type teaser on the cover of the magazine that asked: "Too Busy for Sex?"

My policy is to know a little something about all segments of our society in order to enrich and inform those who manage to squeeze my column in between their advanced studies on social semantics and facial isometrics.

Perhaps it was time to discover something about those who are too busy for sex.

The article is written by Dagmar O'Connor, which is probably a pseudonym for a free-lancing male, and begins by chiding new women for not allowing enough time for "fooling around." It seems to me that's all they do, but I'm here to learn, not argue.

Dagmar goes on to suggest that her busy readers, assuming there is more than one, ought to set up appointments with their loved ones for sex much as they might set up an appointment to have their teeth capped.

She writes: "One evening a week—Wednesday is a nice, neutral day—pick up a bottle of wine and two sandwiches-to-go on the way home from work, and take each other—and the sandwiches—directly to bed."

Sandwiches?

Well, you've got to keep in mind that today's new woman was raised on Big Macs and pepperoni pizza so it doesn't require a gourmet menu to arouse her sexual instincts. If tuna will do it, what the hell. Offer her Chicken Delight and she'll probably bring a trampoline.

Do not, however, complain to me that Wednesday is a bad day. That's your problem. I'm not going to sit here and work out your calendar, for God's sake. Skip bowling.

Dagmar doesn't care whether you eat first or not, that's strictly up to you. But she does suggest that you might want to read to each other or, possibly, sing campfire songs.

It seems to me the whole thing is getting a little complicated, but to each his own. Bring bongo drums if it fits your style.

The article goes on to offer helpful hints on how to take advantage of that "little fleck of mustard on his chin"—assuming he slobbers when he eats—and whether it is all right to interrupt everything to exchange humorous anecdotes.

Many would argue that it's simply the wrong time to pop up and tell a joke, but I guess there's nothing like a good belly laugh to stimulate the old libido of the new woman. A world of wonder awaits if you can just work it into your schedule.

I realize, first of all, that Dagmar's comments were never intended for me. I am not a woman and I am sure as hell not new, at sex or anything else.

Nevertheless, it seems to me that Dagmar, or whatever his real name is, is going out of the way to institutionalize something that ought to be instinctive.

My wife is very busy and I am very busy, but if I ever suggested setting up a date to hop into the sack with even something as exotic as roast duckling with a peppercorn glaze she would probably have me committed.

If these are among the advances that the woman's movement has gained in its somewhat faltering march to the ERA, then I am right in assuming that a noble cause has bogged down in absurdities.

For most normal people, having sex is simply not the same as, say, having your dog groomed unless, of course, you've got something going with the dog groomer.

There ought to be a little magic to the moment, a quality of breathlessness which, by its very nature, would preclude appointment books and tuna sandwiches.

But what the new woman does in the privacy of either her own bedroom or her own kitchen is not up to me. If that little fleck of mustard on his chin turns her on, *vive le moutarde!*

One hopes, however, that at some point in the dismal mutuality of assertive independence and calendar sex, she might wonder fleetingly whatever became of candlelight and wine.

— 30 —

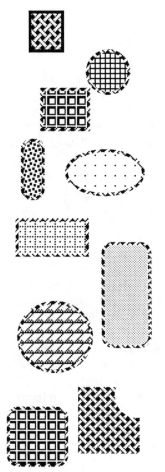

Life in a Cracker Factory

I don't know what would happen, for instance, if I had two complex carbohydrates and no fruit at one meal. I might explode.

© 1986 The Los Angeles Times

I was sitting around the other day discussing triglycerides and complex carbohydrates with my wife when it occurred to me that chamomile tea would probably never replace the simple martini.

The reason we were on the subject is that I have undertaken a special diet which, it is said, may add 10 years to my life. I am not sure, however, it will be the kind of life worth living.

I have entered the program not to join the parade of skinny old men shuffling through town, clinging to life by a thread as tenuous as a strand of linguini, but to get my heart back into the shape it ought to be.

There is nothing like the fear of death to draw one's attention to good nutrition. So follow along as we witness the pathetic descent of a lusty gourmand into the gray world of plain gelatin and buckwheat flour.

The diet basically reduces to a minimum fats and cholesterol-causing foods at my table. Should a cow accidentally wander into the kitchen, I am to kill it instantly and burn the carcass.

Cows in any form, to hear my dietician tell it, are a part of my past.

A typical dinner menu under the prevailing stringent conditions, for instance, will allow me the following for a lip-smacking meal:

One-half cup of skim milk, three small servings of vegetables, one small apple, one ear of corn and 3.5 ounces of fish.

If I am still hungry after that, as surely I will be, I may indulge in "a fun little rice cracker" for nutrition and, I suppose, for laughs.

I have managed to avoid that so far, sparing myself fun with a rice cracker until a more desperate time.

My metabolism, meanwhile, is fueled by a precise blend of proteins, complex carbohydrates, fruits, vegetables and fat-free dairy products in such fine balance that I am afraid to tamper with it.

I don't know what would happen, for instance, if I had two complex carbohydrates and no fruit at one meal. I might explode.

The possibility is haunting. The other day I was about to sit down to a bowl of delicious cardboard-flavored vegetarian chili and lima beans cooked in rain water when I suddenly began to wonder, God help me, if my chili was clashing with my lima beans.

It's sad to see a grown man accustomed to the hearty enjoyment of *poitrine de veau* abruptly in a panic over his vegetarian chili, but there I was, going down a list of food-exchanges on a card from my pocket to see if the nutritional balance was proper.

"Easy," my wife said, when she noticed I was beginning to perspire.

"Easy, hell," I said. "I may be creating deadly chemistry in my body by mixing chili and lima beans."

"You're overreacting to a simple program of nutrition."

"There is nothing simple about this diet," I said. "I am supposed to have green sapsago cheese and no sorbitol or manitol." I leaned closer. "I don't even know what the hell sorbitol and manitol are."

"Poor dear," she said.

I have committed myself to this Spartan existence for a month and have pretty much abided by the unforgiving menu, with the possible exception of last night when I said to hell with my triglycerides and drank a dry vodka martini. Well, actually, two. And I didn't feel a damned bit guilty about it.

My poor attitude strikes at the very core of the program.

I was warned at its outset that the most important part of the regimen was a positive mental approach.

"That," my wife said later, "is going to be your Achilles' heel."

Possibly. For example, I am emotionally incapable of carrying a can of unsweetened baby food or a "grain beverage," whatever the hell that is, to a restaurant in order to maintain my program of good nutrition while dining out.

I am further incapable of "speaking up with appropriate restaurant suggestions when in a group," insofar as those suggestions might encompass a cheerful call for cooked Wheatena or another round of unsalted eggplant.

I'd rather eat dog than eat eggplant.

However, I do understand the importance of good food at this faltering stage in my life, so a plate of Chinese cabbage, cooked celery and unflavored broccoli will do me no harm, though I must remember to go easy on foods containing oxalic acids.

There is no point in a healthy heart if I O.D. on beet greens.

Nevertheless, I have, as I mentioned, remained reasonably true to my health program with that one slippage into the ugly swamp of vodka and vermouth.

It happened in a bar called Tail O' the Cock.

"You're ordering a martini?" my wife asked, surprised.

"Right," I said. "But, and this is important, *no olive.* The olives are deadly."

"Booze is deadly."

"All right," I said, "I'll have a martini, you have chamomile tea."

She thought about that for a moment and then said, "One margarita, with salt, hold the straw."

We had such a good time, we skipped the rice crackers.

— 30 —

NATURE

Ashes in the Rain

Life is no willow in the wind, my friends, but a great howling force that can survive the fiery holocausts, a miracle of tenacity and restoration that will not be denied, not ever.

I stood at this very place last October on a trail that looked toward the ocean, when the trees were black and the earth still smoking.

Fire of awful intensity had burned through the Santa Monica Mountains, and one could not avoid the impression that the whole world had died in flames, and nothing would ever grow again where the soil itself still smoldered.

But I had forgotten the strengths of life that lie in the land.

When I returned last weekend to the once-smoking slopes of Charmlee Park, I was therefore amazed to see what rain and time and the wondrous nature of revival had accomplished in the hills above Malibu.

Isolated patches of green grass gleamed like emeralds in the rain, wet with the storm that had just passed through, isolated by diagonals of sunlight streaking through the dark and heavy clouds.

Wildflowers glowed with hues of lavender, pink and gold, ribbons of almost luminescent brilliance that wound among the dips and curves of Encinal Canyon, too bold and breathtaking to seem real.

But there is a wonder here even beyond beauty, a perfect natural mechanism to assure an abundance of life where the earth once seemed lifeless.

Consider the purple phacelia.

It especially glowed in a kind of mist-shimmering radiance along the south-facing slopes of the mountains, with color of such intensity that its petals seemed to vibrate in the mottled sunlight, revealing tones and depths the eye does not instantly perceive.

The phacelia is a native plant, but more than that it is a fire-follower, its seeds germinating quickly in burned-over soil, fed by nutrients from the ashes themselves, pushing up through the charred earth to dress the land with rainbows and to prove once more that life is a powerful condition.

194

I was told all this as I stared like a child at the awesome beauty of the wildflowers growing among the still-charred laurel sumacs, whose bare and blackened branches reached like fingers from the grave toward an iron-gray sky.

"Life will not be held back," a woman I know only as Daphne announced to those of us who had gathered on the slope to hike with the California Native Plant Society. "It will burst right through."

For me, that's the wonder of it. Life is no willow in the wind, my friends, but a great howling force that can survive the fiery holocausts, a miracle of tenacity and restoration that will not be denied, not ever.

The French playwright Jean Giraudoux was right when he said a flower is the perfect poetry of reproduction.

One saw it everywhere in Charmlee Park, from the glowing purple radiance of phacelia in the storm light to the clumps of emerald green at the crown of the blackened oak trees.

"Have you ever seen anything like it?" Daphne asked. "Have you ever seen anything like it in your life?"

I wondered as I stood by the fire trail whether the Easter story of resurrection itself was rooted in the wonder of rebirth that lies in the clockwork of nature, a way of explaining a beauty which, almost 2000 years later, still seems unexplainable.

Did they witness a devastation beyond their ability to understand? Did they despair in a winter of pain and destruction that spring would ever come again, only to watch the ancient wildflowers push through the rain-drenched soil?

Did they translate the resurgence of new life into a tidier religious concept to embrace a miracle too large, too awesome, too beautiful and too complex to otherwise define?

I think so.

I experienced that feeling here on the hillside in the rain as a new storm whispered in from the sea and as new life touched the mountains with pastel, where once the blast-furnace firestorms had come down the Santa Anas to set the trees flaming and the soil smoldering.

This is, after all, what we are all about, the carriers of life forward past the fires to a yet undefined goal, enhanced by nutrients of the spirit to bring beauty back to the burned fields.

The hike was over. The day was too wet and cold to tramp about in, but it didn't matter. For me, the walk had begun and ended where the purple wildflowers grew, where the forces of life proved once more too much for an arsonist's madness.

Someone, I don't know who, said, "God gave us memory so we would have roses in winter."

And wildflowers to ponder the quintessential mysteries of the beauty that follows calamity.

— 30 —

Days of Amber Sunlight

I ask him why she cries.

He puts his arms gently
around her and as he
leads her away he says,
"She's just crying for
everybody."

*What stays in mind is the odd, flat sunlight, amber
tinted through a thin layer of smoke, and the woman
who stands alone in the middle of an empty road, crying.*

*I see her from a perspective oddly softened by the
hazy light, like the face of an aging actress misted by
a kindly lens.*

*I stop and ask if everything is all right and she says
yes through a voice choked with sobs. I ask if her
home has been burned and she shakes her head no.*

*I stand in that strange light on a day the whole world
is burning, wondering what to do for her, when a
man approaches through the smoke and I ask him
why she cries.*

*He puts his arms gently around her and as he leads
her away he says, "She's just crying for everybody."*

Fire is an awesome adversary.

Only up close, where smoke clogs the lungs and heat sears the
face, can one perceive the immensity of the enemy roaring and
howling down the mountainside, red-flamed and dark-smoked.

Only up close, head tilted back to gauge height, is it possible to
imagine how much courage and discipline it requires to stand firm in
the face of such an enemy and to meet it with nothing more terrifying than a hose shooting water.

October is the cruelest month.

Santa Anas blow with wild caprice across the Southern California deserts, draining moisture from the overheated air and trans-
forming the dry mountains into mounds of fuel waiting to be ignit-
ed.

On Monday, they were.

Grass and scrub brush and trees burned with the ferocity of
magnesium in the lunatic winds that danced and whirled up the hillsides and down the canyons.

Flames leaped highways and ate through homes and threatened to burn the very sea itself.

Decker Canyon, Piuma Canyon, Tapo Canyon, Peach Hill, Box Canyon, Mt. Gleason, Wheeler Canyon, Hummingbird Hill.

I wandered through them at the height of the firestorms because it isn't good enough to view disaster from a distance when you're a reporter, and that's what I'll always be.

"I wouldn't go up there," a highway patrolman said to me at the foot of Encinal Canyon.

"Pass this barricade at your own risk," another said to me at the eastern blockade of the Simi Valley Freeway.

I take minimal risks, but I had to experience the hot winds on my face and cough up the black soot and stand eyes watering on the edge of the red wall of flames, because it was about time I felt what the firefighters felt.

"Isn't this some kind of living?" one of them said to me, hunched away from the flames, trying to clear his lungs. Fire and sweat blackened his face. He was no older than my son.

"Maybe you ought to look for an office job," I said.

"What?" he replied in mock indignation, "and give up the healthy outdoors?"

Firemen are special people.

There were armies of them in hats and heavy yellow jackets through the Santa Monica, Santa Susana and San Gabriel Mountains, working through the bellowing nights and into the angry days, holding a fire line here, losing a battle there.

I watched them stand against overwhelming odds to save homes in Decker Canyon and march into the flame and smoke that cast the amber light at high noon over Hummingbird Hill.

I saw them marshal for the fight in Malibu, a dozen trucks parked down the center of Pacific Coast Highway, where fire had already leaped the road and singed the landside trees of the ocean-side homes.

The trucks and the men were the dividing line between calamity and serenity, for, even as the canyons died, sun-worshipers played on the beach, laughing bicyclists pumped down Pacific Coast Highway and, incredibly, runners jogged among the smoky ruins.

If I ever doubted that Malibu would endure forever, I don't anymore.

I say that, however, without rancor. Small sanities maintain the balance in great disasters. God gave us sunshine in winter to remind us that spring would come again.

Not everyone jogged and not everyone sun-bathed and not everyone rode their 10-speeds among the fire trucks.

Strangers worked to save the homes of people they didn't know, and then moved on to do what they could to fight a fire that didn't affect them.

A different kind of empathy lured spectators to the overpasses of the Simi Valley Freeway to watch the clusters of China-red flames among the boulders of the Santa Susanas, like a theatrical audience at a Dantesque performance.

Disaster, in its way, is the ultimate form of visual gossip, full of shouts and whispers, at once mysterious in its message and awesome in its portent.

Fire burning through the mountains from the canyons to the sea is front page and prime time, something to measure our lives against, close enough to observe but distant enough to be harmless.

I'm not saying we don't care. We do.

"Most people aren't without feeling," a fireman said to me. "They're just glad it's not their home burning.

> *And there's the woman in the amber sunlight*
> *surrounded by billows of smoke against the*
> *flame-clusters, against the immensity of fire,*
> *against a whole world burning.*
>
> *She cries for all of us.*

— 30 —

One
Cat
Dancing

**The gray cat will dance
again, my friends. She
only waits resting in the
corners of the forest,
where the wind hides.**

The wind came like a ghost in the night, flying out of quiet places, full grown and wild. With it rode a kind of breathless exhilaration that set the world in motion. Trees bent and broke, leaves spun in ghostly eddies, wires snapped and popped like fireworks. Little boys on their way to school threw back their heads, flung out their arms and caught the gale in their faces, tasting the distance. A gray cat leaped and bounded through the howling air.

It was a rare and cleansing few days, a time of excitement even as it was a time of danger. Storm quickens the senses. Winds of fury shrink large problems to proportionate size. The world is suddenly lit with new perspectives.

We grow in high winds, when the cat spins and dances over the flatlands and down the canyons. Values shift when the lights go out, when the television set goes silent, when the phone won't work. We turn to each other and listen to the banshee sounds.

I know the hazards of the rushing Santa Anas. I live in a canyon and more than once have sniffed the flaming brush, hot smells carried from a distant arson. I have seen the high flames coming, suddenly a bright orange cat, eyes burning, howling and dancing on a distant mountainside. This wind was no different. Homes died in the calamitous night, memories lay in charred and smoking heaps.

We can make no peace with the elements. Twice I have stood on my rooftop while the hot winds blew and the orange cat danced closer. Ten times twice I have sandbagged the road and plugged the leaks and cursed the lightning. Someday I may be a storm-witness to my own destruction.

But still . . .

When the gale came, I walked and drove through the canyons and along the oceanfront. A heavy oak tree snapped in the windstorm and went down like a wounded giant in a shower of leaves. Twigs flew through the air. The branches of the big oak waved like human arms in a final death throe. A metal garbage can clanging down the street sang the dirge.

The swirling, white-capped ocean swept me back to the Sea of

202

Japan 30 years ago aboard a troop ship in a typhoon. It was the first time I had come face to face with the wild power of nature, a young Marine sentry strapped to the metal of the rolling, heaving transport whose size had so abruptly diminished in the grip of the storm. I was riding a toy I had thought was a monster.

I remember being more awed than afraid, drenched by the waves that crashed over the bow, gasping for breath in the wild wind, abruptly an integral part of the furious night, thinking I would never see anything like it again . . . .

Fear was a growing secondary emotion until an old gunnery sergeant suddenly lurched from the darkness like an element of the storm—somehow, though unfettered by safety lines, keeping his balance in all the craziness around us, grinning across a wet cigar clamped in his teeth.

"You all right?" he asked, swaying with the motion. I said I was. He nodded then said, "Compared to this, everything else is pissin' in the wind." Then he was gone.

It wasn't quite that way last week, standing by my car along Pacific Coast Highway. No war awaited when the sky lay still again. There was, to the contrary, a festival feeling among those who had gathered one by one or in couples to watch the ocean splash and spray and to feel the embrace of the gale. Young men shouted bravely. Young women laughed. The wind carried their messages aloft.

Cats dancing, yowling.

In the cities of West L.A., broken wires whipped and snake-danced over the streets, yet one more testimony to the fragile strands of communication that bind us together. A line went down in front of our house and two exhausted firemen studied it for a moment like children watching ribbons in a breeze. They determined it was harmless and left. The line danced with the cat until the party ended.

It did end. All parties do. The weekend glowed without memory of the wind. Silver is the gift of calamity, lacing the day after.

I walked and drove the same route on the weekend. Sure, it was spring in January, the kind of sweet-tasting day weathermen roll their eyes over. Sails flapped at the Marina del Rey. Women pranced, men postured. There was a kind of low cool to it all, a parade of the plastic sun-soldiers.

But these aren't the storm-people, however they might be enjoying the cosmetic rituals of the singles beaches. These are fair weather weekenders with fair weather goals and fair weather values. No storms blow through their lives. No trees bend.

All right. I don't begrudge yellow days or starry nights. To each his own temple. But, given a choice, leave me to the nights the gray cat dances, to the days that whip with anticipation: *someone's coming, something's happening.*

Southern California wallows in its listless sunny days. There is a kind of endlessness to the summer glare, a chill of the spirit to the air conditioning. The land cracks, flowers die.

But I can wait out the caprice of seasons, knowing the whimsical nature of weather. The gray cat will dance again, my friends. She only waits resting in the corners of the forest, where the wind hides.

— 30 —

When the Scary Winds Blow

They come whispering
in off the desert, hot
and dry and dangerous,
sucking the moisture
from the air and sending
temperatures climbing
steadily up the scale, like
the rising intensity of a
silent scream.

There's a stillness to the hours that precede them, a time when the whole world seems to wait. The dry grass stands motionless on the hillsides, and not a leaf of the oak trees moves. Mountain dwellers nervously study the horizon and firemen fuss over their equipment. The very air crackles with tension. The wait feels endless.

Then the first winds blow.

They come whispering in off the desert, hot and dry and dangerous, sucking the moisture from the air and sending temperatures climbing steadily up the scale, like the rising intensity of a silent scream.

Their entry into the Valley, at first timid brushes with the highest branches, soon builds to howling frenzy, and the winds fly through the fields and the canyons with a madness that matches their unpredictability, full of wild mischief and sudden bursts of temper.

A friend calls them the crazy ladies, firemen see them as the devil winds, we know them as the Santa Anas.

As we have seen, autumn is their time of year, when the pressure builds in the north and drops in the southwest and the crazy ladies come rushing downhill through a door flung open at the Mojave by the dynamics in the atmosphere 20,000 feet up.

And they dance with a speed that sets the world on fire.

I was born in a thunderstorm, stood combat watch in a typhoon and wrote stories in a hurricane, but I've never seen winds quite so strange and scary as the Santa Anas.

I suppose a part of that is the quality of uneasiness that precedes their arrival and the caprice of their manner when they arrive. Trees bend first to the south and then to the west and then spin like witches at a ritual as *las mujeres locas,* the crazy ladies, dance by.

"You always know when they're coming," a county fireman said to me. "Everyone is on edge, you know? There's something in the air, an energy or an electricity, that sets your hair bristling. All you can do is stand watch and wait."

And when they do come, the fire bells almost always ring. They're beginning to ring already for the Santa Monica Mountains, and no one knows where they'll ring next. For along with the caprice of the gales comes the arsonist with the torch, responding to the special tensions the devil winds create. Like the crazy ladies that dance to a music of their own, the fire-starter reacts to a passion in his head that only an inferno will satisfy. The love affair is a strange and fiery union.

"The Santa Anas become more dangerous every year," the county fireman said. "Not because they're any stronger or any more frequent, but because of where people are building their houses. When I first began fighting fires around here 28 years ago, you could burn 50,000 acres and not come anywhere near a home.

"Now there are almost always structures involved. The open spaces are going fast."

I'm a canyon dweller. When the mornings are sweet and the nights at peace with the owls and the coyotes, I can well understand why I chose to build my house among the oak trees. Even when it rains so hard you can't see your way up the hill, I'm glad I'm where I am and don't mind the buckets that catch the water dripping through leaks in the roof.

Only when the Santa Anas come whirling through the passes that link them to the desert, and tendrils of smoke in the distance become firestorms in my neighborhood do I stand like a peacemaker in a war zone, wondering at the prudence of my position.

Fire creates a calamity all its own. Stirred to savagery by the crazy ladies, it quickly becomes a catastrophe that leaves lives and timbers smoldering on the mountainsides, awesome reminders of the elemental nature of our environment. Live with the trees, die with the trees. Stake your claim and take your chances.

"There are three things you can do to help," the county fireman said. "Clear your brush and trim away your dead branches." The third? "Move."

The ideal situation, I suppose, would be to have no houses at all in the mountains and on the hillsides, so that the fire and the wind could simply dance themselves out in the dry chaparral without endangering anything man-made. When homes are involved, the fireman's job becomes more dangerous than it already is, for then he must extend himself beyond safety to preserve what we've built where we shouldn't have built it.

But the ideal is rarely achieved, and we are left to rely on the firefighter's bravery to stand with inadequate weapons between us and the forces of nature that periodically come to slap us around for the sake of diversion.

The winds of danger are here now. As I look out the window, high branches bend, leaves fly past and dust whirls across an open field. The air is swept clean of smog, and the pristine distance fakes the eye into believing the mountains are close enough to touch. They shimmer in the dry heat.

And the whole world waits for the crazy ladies to dance through.

— 30 —

Dancing
With the
Fire Lady

Nature is not a timid
lady. She flounces into
our lives in a gown of
flames and whirls in the
winds that blow . . . .

I smelled it first, the faint drift of a distant burning, and then as I rounded a curve on Topanga Canyon Boulevard, I saw the glowing red flames clawing at the hot sky and clouds of smoke billowing from the ridge. Then, closer still, the fire's stereophonic basso profundo rushed down corridors of sound, counterpointed by the terrified soprano of a dozen sirens. And finally I was there, looking down at a scene that never ceases to fill me with wonder and respect, a terrible vista of technicolored calamity, all the heart-stopping music orchestrated to full effect: The mountains were burning again.

Nature is not a timid lady. She flounces into our lives in a gown of flames and whirls in the winds that blow through tresses of smoke, a wild and uninhibited dancer in the overheated air, simultaneously dangerous and spellbindingly beautiful. Last week in Topanga Canyon she danced through the afternoon and late into the night, until the awful music finally subsided and only the cleanup crews remained to restore the ruined dance floor and to wonder what madman had invited the lady to a party no one wanted.

Fire, open and uncontrolled, is an awesome force. At its height it seems unstoppable, towering over the small armies of brave men who form thin, vulnerable battle lines on the ground, its flames reaching up to the toy-like planes and helicopters that dip and circle above. One cannot help but marvel at the courage of the soldiers and the pilots who throw themselves into a war that seems impossible to win; they are perishable annoyances in the path of the dancing lady.

I watched them through an afternoon that was already unbearable in the 100-degree heat of the day and which seemed impossible to endure against the added scorching winds of the fire. Even far away from the searing core of the battle I could feel the heat sting my face and wondered, my God, how do they do it, *why* do they do it? *For the same reason a man will deliberately step into a bullet meant for a friend or a mother throw herself into the path of a speeding car to save a child.* There is something good in us, something strong, something beautiful.

Firemen do not rank among the masters of articulation. I didn't expect poetry when I asked a few of them why any adult in his right mind would want to be part of a profession that ranks among the most dangerous in the nation. Little boys want to be firemen but grown-ups ought to know better. It doesn't pay a hell of a lot, the hours aren't terrific and the hazards can, in the flicker of a shifting wind, quickly prove terminal.

The best answer, I guess, came from an exhausted young man who simply said he wanted to help. He had been a cop for a while but, to him at least, carrying a gun wasn't helping anyone. Carrying a hose was. I asked him who it was he wanted to help and why. He looked at me with the expression of a man too tired and busy to talk to another damned fool reporter asking another damned fool question and said, "I want to help *the people.* That's what we've got to do, isn't it?"

Not everyone. Not the person, for instance, who probably set the mad lady dancing through the mountains in the first place. One can only guess at an arsonist's rage against the rest of us, at the destructive hostilities that only a firestorm can satisfy. I wondered as I watched the flames eating away at the grass and brush if from some distant vantage point the arsonist was watching too, and it made me both sad and angry to realize that he probably was. Isn't that why he torched the mountains to begin with? To watch?

Later I wandered through the neighborhoods whose residents had waited for the caprice of the winds to spare or destroy them. They stood in clusters before their homes. One or two perched on their rooftops like lookouts against a distant enemy. There were garden hoses and garbage cans filled with water and wet towels in evidence. One man tested his roof sprinklers. Neighbors spoke to one another in muted tones and stared toward the smoke rising in a cloud over them. Ashes fell on their cars.

Had the wind blown south instead of north, they would have been in the fire's path. They knew that. But they also knew, as they have known in the past, that between them and the fiery dancing lady was the young man who wanted to help, and if he could— if anyone could—it would be he who would tell the lady it was time to go home.

The next morning I stood again at the crest of the hill, looking down to where the fire had been. The land was black and charred, except for the blowing white dust of the chemicals dropped from the sky, some of it clinging like Christmas flocking to the darkened fingers of the burned trees, trees with hands half-open in the frozen finality of rigor mortis.

I will not soon forget this warscape, left by the mad lady in her savage dance through the Santa Monica Mountains. And I know she will dance again, at other times and in other places. But I also know that when she does, when the discordant music of her revelry is building to full crescendo, the young man with the simple commitment to help will be there waiting. Turn out the lights, the party's over.

— 30 —

Fire in the City, Fire in the Canyons

Standing small and flammable before a firestorm is bearing witness to a different god . . . .

Already small brush fires burn China-red off the road-sides, etching calamity in thin, gray tendrils of smoke against cloud-less skies. Already warning signs are up along winding canyon thoroughfares, bleak portents of deadlier days to come. Already fire departments are on special alert, already tall weeds, so recently green, lie dangerously dead and golden against bone-dry hillsides, already a fear of a distant arson rides the winds. Dangers shimmer in the hot canyon air. *Something's coming.*

A firestorm is an awesome enemy, bearing down with full flame and fury, flashing brilliant colors against the horizon. It wraps the world in the roar of a thousand jet engines, towering above the tallest trees, searing, choking and blinding. Standing small and flammable before a firestorm is bearing witness to a different god, and knowing how harsh his judgment can be.

I say all this by way of preparing you for the disasters predicted this brush-fire season, already upon us. I know you don't need warning, because it doesn't take a fireman or a scientist to tell anyone that the Santa Monica Mountains are dry for burnin', and that one small spark can light the torch of a million personal disasters. Memories melt to wet ash in a twinkling of the time it took to build them and deaths are mourned in the crematory fires of Armageddon.

The very *anticipation* of a firestorm lays an uneasy stillness over the mountains. You stop suddenly in your tracks and sniff the air. You study the horizon. You listen. *Is something out there?* The question lingers all season in the hot, dry air.

Then why, for God's sake, does anyone live in canyons?

Funny you should ask. I've lived in one for 17 years, through flame and flood and sliding earth, and I'm still not sure why. Twice I have stood against the sky-tall firestorms and more times than that against drenching rains and mud-waters flashing through the living room. And each time afterward I have said to myself, *This is it, no*

214

more, back to the city. But I can't go back. The silence keeps calling.

Whatever disasters lie ahead are lost in the layers of serenity that drape our canyon on a glowing spring night. Walking down a mountain trail beyond the lights and beyond the far hum of traffic is to lose one's self in another world of coyote wail and night bird song. Depths of silence, measured in feet, mute travail the way water mutes sound. Stress fades in a dark wake. So close to the city, so far from chaos.

But still . . . .

Friends argue that I can live in a safe place and walk in an artsy wonder whenever the mood takes me, by the simple expediency of a car. Buy a house where the firestorms don't visit and drive to the canyon quiet when the need for stillness becomes an ache in my soul. But is there a safe place? Truly safe?

I've lived beyond the trees only to face violent shadows in the streets and burglar sounds at the windows. I've had houses that wouldn't slide in areas where it didn't rain only to endure neighbors who didn't think. I have had street lights instead of moonlight burning through my windows, and sirens instead of coyotes howling down the alleys. Lights everywhere. Cops everywhere. Double locks on the doors. Guard dogs in the yard.

At least there is elemental caprice to the direction of a firestorm. It doesn't want *me*. It wants whatever lies in its path to clean-burn the earth for future change, the way a storming ocean claws at the homes along the seashore, reducing a whole human structure to flotsam and jetsam, without even a pause to measure market value. Neither firestorm nor ocean storm equate victims in terms of social standing. Blacks, whites and browns drift on equal tides.

Not so the figures that dart from shadows in hushed footfalls behind you. They stalk the *individual* the way an animal hunts prey, keeping cadence beyond vision, matching pace, relentless in pursuit. I've been there too. Alone and without assistance, I have had to turn and face one of those figures on a dark street, and the fear that rushed through me was far greater than any terror I have known watching flames march down a mountainside. There is a different kind of fire in the city, and it burns like a tiger's eyes in the jungle, with deadly purpose.

So I stay in the canyon despite memories of firestorms, trading the season's uneasiness for snatches of serenity on starry nights, paying in trepidation for one long walk on a lonely trail.

We clear away the brush and trim the trees and check the hoses and install sprinklers on our rooftops. From now until the rains come again, each Santa Ana wind will whisper danger in the mountains as it rustles through the dry grass and sighs in the branches.

We watch the horizon for that first thin, gray tendril of smoke and listen for the high, wailing sirens. Then we will prepare for the fight, knowing how futile our efforts might be, knowing how much we might lose.

Something's coming!
I know it is. But still . . . .

— 30 —

NOSTALGIA
AND
OBSERVATIONS

High on a Hill

Almost every morning
I trudge up the dusty
trail to savor a moment
beyond the clamor, to
sit where the wind
whispers and the sun
rises . . . .

There is a knoll in Topanga State Park, up an oak-shaded back trail, where you can see all the way to the ocean.

If the ridge lines in the opposite direction were lower, it would be possible to see the San Fernando Valley too, simmering in its own heat.

But only at night, when the reflection of its lights glows in the sky over the mountaintops, do you realize the Valley exists at all.

There is a beauty to that too, the brush of city lights against the sky, but if you visit the knoll after sundown, you lose the ocean.

It disappears into the darkness, indistinguishable from the night itself. You can't have both beauties.

Everything is a trade-off.

In any direction, the view of the Santa Monica Mountains is visual poetry, sweeping off into the distance in a symmetry of style and balance that dominates the world from the top of a hill.

And there is a silence on the knoll as sweet as sleep.

Almost every morning I trudge up the dusty trail to savor a moment beyond the clamor, to sit where the wind whispers and the sun rises, contemplating the moments in life that gratify and threaten us all.

The other morning, with dawn beginning to break through the mist that rose from the sea, I was contemplating a threat.

I discovered a few weeks ago that I was vulnerable.

I am speaking not of career or emotional vulnerabilities, because I always knew they existed.

I'm talking about a physical flaw.

I took what started out to be a routine treadmill test and ended up discovering that one of the arteries of my heart was partially blocked.

Subsequent tests revealed that it was not a situation that required surgery, at least not now, but it did demand some life-style changes that, naturally, I was prepared to follow.

It's the trade-off I was talking about.

I have to cut down on cholesterol-causing foods, lose weight and start exercising, which are not requirements likely to cause me great pain.

That isn't what bothers me.

What bothers me is the very notion that I am no longer what I was. What bothers me is a new awareness of the beating of my own heart.

This began, of course, with the revelation of the partial blockage but intensified when I began taking my own pulse during exercise.

Suddenly, that beat was everything, a throbbing confirmation of life that even started pulsing in my ears at night before I went to sleep.

I felt like a player in a Poe drama, hearing the telltale heart throbbing through the house.

I knew I had to deal with that.

Part of my exercise is walking, so I took to trudging up that back trail of Topanga State Park, trying different pathways that cut off from the main route, and it was there I discovered the knoll.

The view before me was almost unreal in its beauty.

I sat on the bald nob of the hill so long the intensifying heat of the day drove me back under an oak tree.

But then I discovered that by seeking shade, I lost the glimpse of the ocean through a break in the ridge line, and impaired that grand and sweeping view of the Santa Monicas themselves.

So what I did in that case was give up a little sleep for view.

I learned that if I got up earlier I could reach the knoll before the sun had a clear shot at it, and I could sit there without need of shade and contemplate with clarity the mist that lay like a silver sheen on the ocean.

Trade-off. I didn't need the sleep. I needed the view.

There is something about the mountains and something about the ocean that places in tight perspective the problems that whirl around us like gnats on a summer evening.

It isn't just the massive thrust of the peaks toward the sun or the almost cosmic sweep of the sea toward its own elusive horizons, but rather a quality of age and endurance that dwarfs our life spans.

Here is something vaster and grander and higher and deeper than I am, something that has lasted through the ages of the Earth into the era of its primates, something wondrous, something breathtaking.

I sat on the knoll for a long time that first day, placing against the immensity of the view the beat of my own heart, and after a while I found I wasn't concentrating on myself anymore.

The small tensions and the burning hostilities faded, if only for that moment, and I could be at peace with that finite portion of the universe, aware only of the wind that touched my face.

That doesn't mean I'm going to join the priesthood or start wearing flowers in my hair, but it does mean that I know a place now where, when I become too conscious of my own heartbeat, I can consider the rhythms of the ocean instead, and the seasons of the mountains.

That's more of a confirmation of life than I ever realized before.

— 30 —

Days
of Drums
and Bugles

His body continues
to fall through my
dreams in a long,
slow spiral that
will never
end.

I dug into a cardboard box in a dark corner of my closet the other afternoon to find the only souvenir I had kept from the Korean War. It is a photograph of me and my best friend at the time, a kid from Greenpoint, Brooklyn named Joe Citera. We were two 20-year-olds decked out in combat gear, trying our damndest to look the part of mean Marines. I had an M-1 rifle and Joe held a .45 he had borrowed for the picture.

Despite our efforts to appear the very epitome of what the Corps used to call "perfect killing machines," the fear and uncertainty of what lay ahead was written in our eyes. As well it should have been. In less than a week, Joe Citera would be dead.

I sat looking at the photograph for a long time, until the light had drained from the sky and the room was in almost total darkness. I was trying to recall the names of others I had known who died in what Winston Churchill once referred to as "the war that can't be won, can't be lost and can't be ended."

But we are three decades removed from those days of drums and bugles, and the names have vanished from my memory as quickly as Joe Citera vanished from my life on a bloody piece of land known only by its numerical designation, Hill 749.

I put the photograph away and said nothing for a long time. I couldn't have talked if I wanted to. There are some griefs that time will never lessen.

I had not consciously thought about the Korean War for years. I say *consciously* because there are still nightmares occasionally, and I know that every terrifying moment of the 15 months spent in combat will be replayed for the rest of my life in a shadowy corner of my mind. I began to see some of them last week after receiving a call from a man named Larry.

He had guessed from earlier references in my column that I might have been in Korea during what everyone in the 1950s was calling the "conflict" or the "police action." He was trying to form a group to lobby for a Washington memorial honoring the 54,000

Americans who had died back then for a cause none of us fully understood. Larry wanted my help.

I left him dangling because the thought of a memorial had not occurred to me before. That afternoon, I dug out the picture of Joe, and in subsequent days tried to piece together the images of what had transpired in Korea and how I had felt about it, like a child trying to recall the terror of a distant thunder. To prod my memory, I stopped off at a small building that houses a counseling center for veterans of the Vietnam War. I wanted to see some artifacts of combat.

The mementos filled one wall of the center: faded black and white photographs, a flak jacket, a helmet, some green berets, a citation for a Purple Heart and another for a Bronze Star, a camouflaged uniform, a dungaree hat, boots.

I studied them for 35 minutes and took notes, but it was only when I touched the helmet that images of a war long ago flashed back. There was the sound of Joe's anguished voice on his dying night, the napalm-charred bodies of enemy soldiers frozen by sudden death in the posture of flight, the explosive disappearance of a Marine not 20 feet away who had stepped on a mine, the brittle winter roar of a thousand mortar shells as they struck like bolts of lightning from an iron gray sky.

I saw a young corporal *(was that me?)*, M-1 ready, at the point of his squad, rounding the bluff of a cliff on a narrow pathway high above an unnamed valley, coming face to face with a North Korean soldier, his automatic weapon at the ready.

There was a split second of stunned immobility, a heartbeat of indecision, and as I studied his face in the still-life of that isolated encounter—a smooth, round face with eyes that shone like polished coal—I remember thinking, *my God, he's only a kid!*

We were trained well, the two of us, and our instincts were honed to survival. We reacted almost simultaneously in a conditioned reflex of two weapons pointed, but only one trigger pulled. I fired first. The enemy soldier (a boy!) disappeared from the cliffside as though he had been jerked from the ledge by a cable. His body continues to fall through my dreams in a long, slow spiral that will never end.

Joe Citera and an unknown North Korean, oddly companionable in the mutual context of their terrible destinies.

It was not my intention to burden anyone with my memories of a war best forgotten, but I did want to explain to a man named Larry, whose last name I didn't even write down, why I will not participate in a campaign that would honor *only* the Americans who died in Korea.

Tribute, if required at all, is due those on both sides for having died so young and so bravely in such a brutal exercise of governmental power over our lives. But, by honoring the dead, we would be honoring their killers, and I don't think I will ever be able to forgive myself (much less honor my deed) for blasting another human being into the long, slow turns of humanity's sad history.

— 30 —

Cat Chow
and Chili
After Dark

Those of us who are night
creatures have a special taste
for that kind of loneliness,
and not necessarily because
we're alone.

Night is the loneliest time, like a stray cat with nowhere to go wandering down an empty street. It's a time when insomniacs tease small problems into red-eyed horrors and the newly divorced reach out next to them and find no one there. Night is a time of abandoned parks and desolate alleys and whole streets without movement. Night is a single light burning in a dark building.

Those of us who are night creatures have a special taste for that kind of loneliness, and not necessarily because we're alone. It's the cat in us. There's a gentling quality to the world after dark when the mail doesn't come and the phone doesn't ring and the whole frantic tempo of the day is a muted drum riff.

Cats wander the small hours as much to *perceive* as to hunt, shadowy curiosities on hushed footfalls at the edge of an urban forest. Cats know the mysteries of the night.

I'm not talking midnights here. I'm talking 3 a.m. to dawn, after the bars are closed and the drunks are gone; when, as Sinatra used to sing, "the world belongs to the cops, and the janitors with their mops . . . ." When even exhausted lovers, their fantasies spent, tumble like tired children into their dreams.

Every once in a while I awaken during those hours, nerves tingling, and hit the streets. This time it was fairly new to me because the streets I wandered were in the San Fernando Valley. I've got to tell you, man, I'm a downtown kid and have never believed that *real* people lived in the Valley.

The Valley was a place for chatty girls with bubble gum brains who hung out around the malls and for middle-aged guys in flowered shirts and hair dyed a funny auburn.

Maybe it *is* that way in the daytime. I haven't decided yet. But night is different. Night equalizes. Night adds mystique to the Valley, like red lipstick on a gray old lady. Night lets the cat prowl free on empty streets.

Take the 24-hour markets, for instance, those little 7-Eleven stores tucked away in strange places off boulevards, down Godforsaken side streets you'd think no one in his right mind would wander after sundown. Take the crying lady.

I stopped by a 7-Eleven to buy cigars just in time for a woman in tears to push past me out the door and run sobbing down the street. I turned to the clerk on duty, a young man named Mark, who was staring toward the door and holding one of those wrapped premade sandwiches, looking like he'd just had a birthday gift turned down.

He noticed me and shrugged and said, "I paid for it, might as well eat it." I asked him what had happened. He told me that the woman, about 35 and not bad looking, had come in off the streets and asked to use the bathroom. Because store policy limits the facilities to employees only, the kid had to turn her down.

"Suddenly," Mark said, "she began to cry." He had started to unwrap the sandwich and stopped. "She was mad at first and told me it was a damned rotten policy, like another door slammed in her face, you know what I mean? She said she had no place to go, no money and nothing to eat. I bought her this." He held up the sandwich to show it was a ham and cheese on white.

"That made her cry harder," he said, sighing. "She said ham and cheese just wouldn't do it for her anymore. That's when you saw her, when she ran out the door. Hell, I was going to let her use the bathroom." Mark rewrapped the sandwich and put it aside. "Man," he said, "that's depressing."

I hung around to watch the night people. They were drawn to shelter like refugees from a war. A tense, solemn cowboy who drank black coffee and played a Pac-Man Junior game against a corner wall, beeping frantic electronic music into the room like a guy shooting down silence. A housewife dressed to kill, wandering up and down the aisles, then buying one roll of Scotch Tape. A big-bellied Chinese guy who bought a bag of Cat Chow and a can of Hormel chili.

"How can you figure a woman getting up out of bed at four in the morning to buy Scotch Tape?" Mark asked, shaking his head. "And the guy with the Cat Chow and the chili? He buys it almost every night."

"You ever ask him why?"

"Naw," Mark said. "It's none of my business. Anyhow, I don't want to know if he eats it." He glanced at the solemn man playing games. "As for *El Creepo,* he never talks," Mark said, lowering his voice. "The guy just plays for hours, then splits. He freaks me out, you know? Like suddenly he's going to explode. Maybe he's just lonely."

He picked up the sandwich intended for the crying lady, studied the label carefully, then tossed the whole thing into a waste basket.

"I hate ham and cheese," he said.

Dawn was still an hour away when I left Mark. He was selling a small cherry pie and a cola Slurpee to a teen-age girl with a spike punk hairdo.

The time of the cat was passing. A garbage truck was clanging down the street. I drove home slowly, thinking about Mark and the crying lady. She was right. Ham and cheese just won't do it sometimes.

— 30 —

Some
Quiet
Places

The commute hour passes, the heavy traffic fades and the quiet returns

An old horse stands under a weeping willow tree on La Tuna Canyon Road, a few miles east of the Foothill Freeway, chewing on hay from a feeder and looking up occasionally to watch the traffic go by.

I've seen the horse before, a dappled gelding that looks too decrepit for anyone to ever ride again but who seems to possess a kind of wisdom of the ages from having lived a long time. He's seen it all before.

Having owned a horse once, I doubt that they have a brain in their heads, but every once in a while I spot one that appears to possess at least an ounce of recognition of what's going on around him. Shorty is one of them.

I don't *know* that his name is Shorty, but he looks like the horse my daughter used to ride through the Santa Monica Mountains and, since I don't know his real name, Shorty will do.

He always seems to be standing under that willow tree, no matter what time of day it is. I stopped once to check him out, but no one was around to answer questions and, since I don't talk to horses, we just looked at each other for a few moments and I left.

It was a result of that exchange of glances, however, that I began to wonder if old Shorty realized that the serenity of the canyon he inhabited might be coming to an end.

The question popped into my head because there is an infinite sadness to old horses and I couldn't help but think that maybe the sadness is a recognition of passing time and fading days, an awareness that things can never be the same for them again.

When I looked at Shorty I was certain he remembered summers when he rode the trails of the Verdugo Mountains, up past the quiet stables and the white clapboard homes, winding through the scrub oaks to the hilltops, the wind in his face and the sun at his back.

Days of youth, days of strength.

I was in the kind of mood that blended time and tranquility, I suppose, because I had been reading that La Tuna Canyon has been

232

"discovered." Land developers are carving out tracts. Builders are revving up their dozers.

This saddens me because there aren't too many quiet places left in Los Angeles, and I'd hate to see this one crammed with fields of houses with red-tiled roofs which, by their very homogeneity, defy the tones of natural beauty around them.

Everyone needs a place to hide, whether it's in a canyon or a room in the house, a place where there is quiet enough to contemplate the dynamics of change around us, unjangled by the furies that haunt the freeways.

I have my place in Topanga Canyon, so I can appreciate what's going through the heads of those in La Tuna Canyon who worry that one of these days soon the builders are going to march in like armies of destruction, and all the serenity will be gone.

No more Shorty and no more weeping willow tree.

We're surrounded by parkland in Topanga, but builders are salivating over what other open spaces remain, and even over the parkland itself. Just because it's park doesn't mean it's safe.

Integrity has never been a big factor in the decisions of those we entrust to guard our future. I'm convinced that, if contractors came along with enough campaign money to sway a legislator, the oak trees would be ripped out tomorrow and condos would go up the next day.

I drove out to La Tuna Canyon the other day, not to see Shorty but to absorb the beauty that surrounds him.

It was late afternoon on a hot day, and the leaves of the eucalyptus trees shimmered under the flattening rays of a descending sun. The foothills lay in misty tones of blue-gray, cascading back into shades that darkened with distance.

La Tuna Canyon seems frozen in time, a blend of homey gardens and horse corrals, with a pace to match the look. The Foothill Freeway borders it on the east and the Golden State is not far away on the west, but the canyon still seems removed from the bustle.

Even cars whizzing by on the narrow road somehow fail to disrupt the bucolic nature of the environment. The commute hour passes, the heavy traffic fades and the quiet returns.

Life remains a slow dance there, despite a quickening tempo to the music over the ridge lines, and late afternoon is the best time to take measure of the pace.

I drove down the quiet streets just to look, rustic roads that lay

at the feet of mountains drying in the blaze of summer. Children
played nearby. A dog barked far off. A horse whinnied.

I absorbed the tranquility and found myself hoping beyond reality that the people who own it will not surrender their peace easily,
though, I fear, surrender it they will.

Shorty was still standing under the willow tree as I drove by,
and I had the feeling that I might never see him again. I hollered
"So long, Shorty," and I swear that he looked up and, in his way,
said goodby.

To me and, perhaps, to life in the shade of a weeping willow
tree that was probably never meant to last forever.

— 30 —

Time
After
Time

Time was racing by,
mocking the small
plans, mapping the
long routes, as light
as a feather, as swift
as a blink.

I was sitting on a hillside at the top of Topanga Canyon Boulevard skipping pebbles down a slope when the thought struck me that skipping pebbles is a reprehensible waste of time.

The more I thought about it, the angrier I became, because I should have been pecking at my word processor instead of idling away the hours in a fool's diversion.

"Damn you," I said to myself. I scowled to think I could treat time so. I glared. I shook my fist. And then I went back to skipping pebbles.

I have dealt with time before, you see. We were competitors once, when I was a boy and time was a thunderclap.

I raced time down the corridors of the years, through the days and into the weeks, breathing the seconds like a wind in my face, my future flying a half-step in the lead.

We had a hell of a time and never got tired.

But age damps old fires, and the race slows at the far turn.

Time doesn't have to sprint ahead anymore because I don't run as often as I did, and I have come to realize anyhow that time is going to win the race, no matter how hard I try.

"Time's glory," Shakespeare wrote, "is to calm contending kings."

Distance mutes the battle sounds. Time dims the images.

That is not to say, however, that I am unaware of my recent languor in time's wake. As the days of the year pass like fireflies in the night, I find a quiet place and consider the unfinished business of my life.

I am not speaking here about the business of writing, although I have a manuscript to polish and a screenplay to complete and an unknown number of essays waiting to be composed. I know I'll do those.

I'm talking about the carpet-cleaning brush on the front seat of my car.

That portion of the brush that holds it to the cleaning machine is worn, necessitating replacement of the entire brush. When the machine is used, the brush flies off and spins across the floor. I volunteered to buy a replacement.

My wife shook her head. "I'll never see the brush again," she said.

It is a small task, equivalent, say, to picking up my clothes at the cleaners or stopping by Gary's for nonfat milk and cat food.

The brush is six inches in diameter and weighs a pound. All I have to do is stop at Ward's repair shop and hand them my brush. I don't even have to speak. They will sell me a new one. I will pay and that will be that.

Easier said than done.

The brush has been on the front seat of my car for eight months. Sometimes I pick it up, study it with new resolve and vow that on Wednesday I will take it in.

"Got the brush yet?" I am asked.

"Wednesday," I reply.

But I'm running out of Wednesdays.

I thought about the brush as I skipped pebbles down the slope. The San Fernando Valley simmered in the late afternoon. A pebble ricocheted off a boulder and came to rest at the foot of some scrub oak. A breeze rustled the grass.

I thought also about a hole I dug in the yard a few years ago. The hole was for a fish pond. I bought the cement, a filtering system, a pump and some tubing.

This pond, I promised myself, will someday grace the cover of Sunset Magazine. Travel agencies will include it in their brochures. Japanese tourists will take pictures of it.

Then I looked up. Time was racing by, mocking the small plans, mapping the long routes, as light as a feather, as swift as a blink.

I stood. I ran. The hole filled with dirt again. Rain hardened the cement, still in bags. I gave the pump away. I was still running in those days. Wednesday was a lifetime away.

What will 1986 hold?

Well, I may get the brush replaced for the carpet cleaner. I think I'll fix the leaks in our roof, though maybe not.

The roof has leaked since 1982. I know exactly where the drips will fall. When the rain starts, I put red and yellow plastic pans in precisely the right places.

When it was pointed out to me that plastic pans, however

brightly colored, are unsightly in such a fine home, I attempted an alternative. I put the pans on the roof.

But the roof is sloped and the pans kept sliding into the dog's yard, terrorizing him. The dog thought God was giving him a sign. *Don't bark after 9 at night!* He gets around it by howling.

When wind whipped the pans away, the roof leaked on the carpet. I couldn't stop the leaks because the pans were in the yard.

When the rain stopped, I thought about shampooing the carpet, but I couldn't. The brush was on my car seat.

Adlai Stevenson said, "All I want to do is sit in the shade and watch the dancers." He was older then, past the years of running, and had come to understand quite well the nature of time.

I thought about that as I sat on the hillside and skipped pebbles over the slope. The day was passing and the lights of the Valley were coming on below.

Pretty soon I couldn't see the pebbles anymore.

Was it Wednesday already?

— 30 —

Killing Time at a Roadblock

What does it take to
bring us together,
snatching at the
small alliances that
form when the wind
howls, or when the
traffic stops.

I am an impatient man, given to fits of pique if the requirements of my life are not met with substantial speed. Time haunts me. I don't miss deadlines, I'm never late for appointments and God help the old lady who tries to muscle in front of me at the supermarket checkout stand. If she isn't willing to fight to the death, she'd better not try shoving her damned dog food ahead of my *Mouton Cadet*.

I mention my impatience only so that you may better understand how I might respond to a 55-minute roadblock. It happened on Topanga Canyon Boulevard where they're digging up the highway to install a new water line. A young man halted me at a barricade to tell me there would be a half-hour delay before I could proceed.

"A delay for what?" I demanded.

"For the digging," he replied.

"To hell with the digging," I said, shifting into low.

He shrugged. "You'll be crushed by the digger."

The way he said it caused me to believe that the possibility existed he might be right. I'm not quite sure what a digger is, but I was reasonably certain I didn't want to be crushed by one.

The next five minutes were spent fidgeting: with papers in my briefcase, with the radio, with things in my wallet. I put the seat back and then up again. I took everything from the glove compartment, then returned it. When there seemed nothing left to do, I sighed and stared out the window.

In a very short time, cars began to line up behind me, stretching back toward Fernwood. The attendant at the barricade dutifully walked the line, informing each driver of the delay. They began getting out of their cars. It wasn't a bad idea. I'd rather pace than sit.

"It's a beautiful morning," an elderly man said, joining me at the roadside. He had been in an old pickup directly behind me. He wore jeans and a plaid shirt. His hair was white.

I looked around. Strings of mist wound through the Santa

Monicas, tracing silver lines against a blue sky. There was a clean snap of autumn in the air. All right, I'd give the old man that. "It's not bad," I said.

"When it rains hard, there's a waterfall comes down the side there," he persisted, pointing to an indentation in the face of the mountain.

A young woman had emerged from her Honda. She wobbled slightly on spiked heels. There were braces on her teeth. "Where?" she asked.

The old man pointed again. "A couple of others form during the storms, but that one's the prettiest," he said.

I had a flash of storm water cascading down the cliffside, splashing in fine spray at the bottom. I must have passed it hurrying to somewhere, and the passing glimpse had imprinted on my memory.

"Are there hiking trails in the mountains?" the young woman asked.

The old man laughed. "Hundreds," he said. "You can hike to the ocean or you can hike to the Valley or you can hike to hillsides filled with wildflowers in the early spring. I've been in the mountains 22 years and still haven't seen all the trails."

The wonder was mirrored in her eyes. "I just got here," she said. "I've never seen anything like this before."

I remember a cool place somewhere above Topanga State Park. I had stumbled on it quite by accident on a summer day groggy with heat. A place sheltered by trees that allowed only a filtered sunlight in. It filled me with a serenity I have never been able to recapture. Now when I think about it, I'm not even sure it was real.

"Did you see the coyote?" A young man in a coat and tie was pointing, calling for the girl's attention. *"There!"*

"I see him!" she cried suddenly.

The young man was pleased. He had been watching her. "They're usually not out in the daytime," he explained. "But with winter coming, I guess they're stocking up on food."

"Watch your cats!" a woman called. Everyone laughed.

Clusters of motorists had gathered along the roadside up the line. Someone took pictures. The delay had become an *occurrence*. It was that way during the last flood in the mountains, when the road to the Valley was out and the power gone. People came out of their houses to talk. Others shared wine by lantern light and cooked over fireplaces.

What does it take to get us talking? What does it take to bring us together, snatching at the small alliances that form when the wind howls or when the traffic stops? We have so little time for each other.

I heard a filtered voice coming over a two-way radio. The attendant at the barricade was holding a walkie-talkie. He listened for a moment then gestured. "OK," he said. "The road's clear. Follow the pilot truck."

I glanced at my watch. Fifty-five minutes had passed. I couldn't believe I had remained still that long without going crazy. Engines started. I saw the girl with the braces on her teeth hand a piece of paper to the young man in the coat and tie. A telephone number? Maybe they'd hike together someday.

I shifted into low. The old man waved as he walked toward his pickup.

"Hey," I called. He turned. "You're right," I said. "It's a hell of a morning."

I was still thinking about the waterfall as we followed the pilot truck down the hillside, and about the cool place in the mountains.

— 30 —

A Little Bottle in the Desert

...they just wanted
someone
to know they had
existed.
They wanted to leave
a history.

The paper is yellowed and crumbles easily into dust if carelessly handled. The pencil writing is faded and often difficult to read. Many of the notes were in fragments when Philip Holmes found them, and had to be Scotch-Taped together in order to restore the essence of their contents.

But when they were, some outings lost in time began to emerge.

Forty-one years is not all that long ago, I suppose, and the chronicles of a family's picnics in the Joshua forests near Gorman are not exactly the Dead Sea Scrolls.

But something delicate and touching comes drifting back through the musty decades and, when placed in the context of war and social revolution, the notes become an innocent, yet oddly powerful, commentary on the endurance of the human spirit in even the most terrible of times.

The notes were in a small bottle that once contained Horlick's malted milk tablets. Holmes discovered it last week while hiking. The bottle was half-buried in the desert. He opened it, saw the notes and realized that, as he put it, "this was something to care about."

Phil and his father spent half the night in their L.A. home piecing the messages together, and what emerged was a gentle history of small family pleasures that began in 1944 and ended 10 years later.

They thought I might be interested. I was.

"Lottie and Freeman," the first note says. It is dated April 27, 1944. World War II is in progress. London and Berlin are in flames. D-Day is little more than a month away.

We begin to meet a close and loving family that later notes identify as the Crandalls. Despite the size and horror of distant events, theirs is an oddly innocent age. Family is important. Marriages last beyond the weekend. Summer nights are made for walking.

There is a compelling sweetness to life on the quiet edges of a world at war.

"Lottie and Freeman. Bernie, Joel and me." The year: 1945. Franklin D. Roosevelt dies. The United Nations is created. The Atomic Age is born. The note says: "It is raining."

Later, impishly: "The way to the hiding place is this: Past the camel's knee/In the broken tree/Are the names of the/Sweethearts three."

Then 1946. The world is trying desperately to recover. Atonement is in the air. Nuremberg exacts its punishment. Winston Churchill warns of communism's Iron Curtain. "Ma and I ate dinner here today in the car," the note says. The first American missile is built. Through all the cataclysmic wrenchings of war and warnings, the notes reflect life's fullness through the eyes of Lottie May Crandall when she writes, "All is well. God is good."

The day is Thanksgiving, 1947. The morning is misty. One can see her standing on a desert hill, looking eastward to where the sun is an orange blur through the damp fog.

She gazes at a terrain of slopes and quick rises and then turns from the vista to write: "Pa and I came up the ridge to eat lunch and find our notes. They are OK. But they are clearing up the Joshua forest so fast. It may be gone in time . . . ."

The '40s pass, the '50s come. Korea, the Cold War, Joe McCarthy, the hydrogen bomb, tranquilizers, the birth of the civil rights movement. America sings, "If I Knew You Were Comin' I'd've Baked a Cake."

"Ate lunch at Tumble Inn campground on the old Ridge Route. Hid notes by the stone steps. That's all. Goodby for now. Joel Crandall, Murl, Bernie, Freeman, Gary, Grandma."

I'm not sure why I am moved by observations that emerge from the past like candlelight from the distant darkness. I suppose it's because there's a tug to remember our own childhoods of easy days on sunny hillsides, of family rides through fields now covered with homes, but once lighted by the glory of nature's colors.

"This is the first time I have ever been over Spunky Canyon. We are enjoying the wildflowers very much. Came with grandma and grandpa. Joel Crandall." April 5, 1952.

Then: "We three. The first in '53. Bernie, Joel and Murl. Well, here I am again. Past the camel's knee in the broken tree. Am having a very good time."

The last note says simply: "April 3, 1954. Lottie, Bernie, Gary."

Phil and Les Holmes had to know why the outings ended. A search through telephone books led to Sun Valley's Jackie Warwick. Murl was her father, Gary and Joel her brothers. All are dead. So are Grandma and Grandpa. Time passes. Lives end, lives begin.

Bernie is Jackie's mother and still lives with the memory of those weekend outings in the Joshua forest, where the sun rises over the desert mountains.

Jackie says they just wanted someone to know they had existed. They wanted to leave a history.

The Crandalls might have accomplished more than that. Jim Croce once sang, "If I could save time in a bottle . . . ."

In some small way, through images evoked by faded words on brittle paper, they did just that.

— 30 —

A View
From
Below

A Ferris wheel is, by
necessity, a smooth
and compelling flow
of circular movement,
touching places in
memory that no roller
coaster ever could.

There is something about a Ferris wheel that lures me to the carnival, whether it is tucked into a corner of a county fair or blazing with lights in the middle of a parking lot.

I am drawn to it from a shadow of childhood memory that regards the Ferris wheel as a symbol of special pleasures, an almost mystical circle in the sky, evoking ghosts with the efficacy of a hypnotist's pendulum.

So it was no surprise last week on a morning laced with mist that I was drawn to the Santa Monica Pier, whereupon the new Ferris wheel sits.

Let me say at the outset that it doesn't take a lot to lure me to the ocean. I have an almost primitive response to the sea. I can stand for hours on an isolated beach just staring at the surf, without a thought in my head or the slightest need to communicate with anyone.

I'm happy at the ocean on days of howling storm or withering heat, when wise men rush for shade and shelter, leaving fools to dream on the shoreline.

I don't need a reason to be there. The whisper of a salt-water wind is enough. But a Ferris wheel, like perfume in a woman's hair, adds to the allure, and spins a spell that is hard to resist.

I was southbound on Pacific Coast Highway when I first saw the big wheel turning slowly through strands of fog that lay like silver ribbons over the morning pier.

I was late for a meeting that offered immense column possibilities, but I stopped anyhow to watch the Ferris wheel across the triangle of water that separated us, and eventually I said to hell with the meeting and drove to the pier.

Everyone ought to be able to do that once in awhile, indulging the simple pleasure of recalling with difficulty the childhood freedoms we once thought we would never forget.

Everyone ought to be able to say to hell with it and not end up paying a price beyond the worth of the product.

Weekdays don't draw huge crowds to the pier, so I could sit alone on a bench and watch the Ferris wheel turn without the necessity of making small talk with someone sitting next to me. I've never been good at chatting.

I haven't ridden a Ferris wheel for years, partly because being turned on a wheel through the air is not high on my list of priorities and because, well, riding in a Ferris wheel, like climbing a tree, belongs to other times and other ages.

Watching the Ferris wheel is enough for me, seeing it turn almost silently against a lacy sky, without the clattering roar that accompanies a roller coaster or the uneven rhythms of those other rides that bump and jerk across the sand or sawdust.

A Ferris wheel is, by necessity, a smooth and compelling flow of circular movement, touching places in memory that no roller coaster ever could. A Ferris wheel is for quiet times.

I probably could have sat there alone all day without talking to anyone, but was distracted by a little boy who walked up to within three feet and stared silently into my face.

Kids have a way of doing that. They peer directly into your eyes and wait, knowing with absolute certainty that eventually you are going to do something that no one has ever done before, and they are going to be there to witness it.

I decided not to say anything to the kid as long as he didn't say anything to me. I watched the Ferris wheel and he watched me, waiting for geese to fly from my ears, or my head to explode in a burst of confetti.

"Are you going to ride the Ferris wheel?" he finally asked.

"Maybe," I said.

"My name is Fred."

"Maybe, Fred."

"I'm not afraid of the Ferris wheel," he said.

"Neither am I," I said.

"Then why don't you ride it?"

I was tempted to reply because it might break loose and roll into the sea, but this would have opened a whole new line of questioning, so I just said, "Maybe I will."

"When?"

"Maybe next Monday."

Perfect. I have a friend named Travis who is 4 and who, when he's not sure how to respond, says "Maybe next Monday."

"What's happening next Monday?" Fred wanted to know.

"Everything," I said, which seemed consistently vague.

Fred considered that for a moment and then said, "I'm 6, how old are you?"

"A lot older than 6," I said.

A woman in the distance called his name.

"Well," he said, "I've got to go."

He ran toward her, and moments later they climbed into a seat on the Ferris wheel. Fred saw me and waved enthusiastically from high overhead and I waved back, wishing for a moment that time could transport me to his place, but knowing that it couldn't.

It just isn't the same when your hair is gray and the wonder's gone.

I sat there for a long time watching the Ferris wheel turn. It wasn't until the morning mist had vanished and teen-age boys who called each other "dude" were swarming over the pier that I decided it was time to leave.

But I'll go back again soon to sit on a bench and watch the Ferris wheel and maybe talk to Fred, if he's there. It'll be on one of those to-hell-with-it kinds of days.

Next Monday maybe.

— 30 —

In the
100 Aker
Wood

Pooh is about you
and me and that
cognac-colored
moment when a
scent of memory
sends us flying
back through time
to a place in youth
where, for a perfect
instant, nothing is
wrong.

You get to the 100 Aker Wood by going past the Floody Place and past Where the Woozle Wasn't and past Pooh's Trap for Heffalumps.

Pretty soon, before you know it, you're near where Rabbits Frends and Raletions live and then, at last, Owls House.

And that, my friend, is the 100 Aker Wood.

But why, you ask, would anyone want to go there?

To visit Pooh, silly!

Actually, it's the Hundred *Acre* Wood, but neither Pooh nor Christopher Robin are terrific spelers, I mean spellers, so you have to use your imagination sometimes.

But then, isn't imagination what Winnie the Pooh is all about?

Of course.

And if you have to ask "Where's imagination and how can I touch it?" just remember what Christopher Robin once very wisely remarked when he was halfway down the stairs (which is where he always sat):

"It isn't really anywhere, it's somewhere else instead."

Everyone visits Pooh sooner or later.

Pooh is more than a series of poems and stories about Kangas House and Eeyores Gloomy Place (which is Rather Boggy and Sad) and the un-bouncing of Tigger and the search for Baby Roo when he gets lost.

Pooh is about you and me and that cognac-colored moment when a scent of memory sends us flying back through time to a place in youth where, for a perfect instant, nothing is wrong.

Pooh is about the sweetness in our lives, and while I am more Eeyore than Piglet, the sweetness brushed like a breeze against my face one night at the Coronet Theatre in West Los Angeles.

For an hour or so a British actor named Peter Dennis read from the works of A.A. Milne in a program called "Bother!" which, of course, is what Christopher Robin says when things aren't quite right.

But it was more than a reading.

252

It was a walk through the 100 Aker Wood (past the Bee Tree and the Sandy Pit Where Roo Plays) with a man who resembles everyone's kindly uncle and may even have been Christopher Robin's father, if you can imagine that Christopher Robin's father wore a polka-dot bow tie.

Dennis has been the voice of Pooh for more than a decade, and brings to this remarkable one-man show a quality that goes beyond professionalism into an area we can't even begin to define.

I almost didn't go to the performance. I can't remember why. I had something else to do or I didn't feel like it or there was a show on television I wanted to see. Maybe I had the flu.

But my wife said, "Oh, no you don't."

I said, "Oh, no I don't what?"

"I have been dragged by you to the worst movies of my generation and you are not, I repeat *not,* going to get out of this by staying home to brood or write or vomit."

"Suppose I die?"

"I'll have your body shipped to the Coronet."

Did I mention she's a Pooh fan? I mean a Pooh *fan.*

She has two 50-year-old Pooh books she would kill to protect.

Her license plate is a variation of the note Christopher Robin leaves on his door when he isn't home. The note says "Bisy Backson." The license reads BZ BK SN. And she can quote from memory about half the passages in any Pooh book.

So I said, "OK, I'll go, but I deny ever having taken you to see a bad movie."

"' The Incredible Melting Man'? 'The Fly'? . . ."

"Well, maybe those two."

". . .'Attack of the Killer Tomatoes'? 'Godzilla Meets . . . .'"

"All right, all right. I'll go."

I'm glad I did.

The enchantment of an evening in the 100 Aker Wood was escape in its kindest sense, a brief removal from the pains and stresses that wrench our emotions from dawn to sunset, and sometimes into the shadows of our dreams.

"Wherever I am," Peter Dennis begins, "there is always Pooh."

Then he reads, "'I'm never afraid,' said Pooh, said he, 'I'm never afraid with you.'"

I listened in rapture and admiration as Piglet did a Very Grand Thing on a blustery day, and Eeyore had a birthday and everyone wondered what Tiggers liked to eat.

"'Don't *you* know what Tiggers like?' asked Pooh.

"'I expect if I thought very hard I should,' said Christopher Robin, 'but I thought Tiggers knew.'"

What shall we do about poor little Tigger?

If he never eats nothing he'll never get bigger.

It was a special evening, and a few days later I talked about it to one of my best friends. His name is Travis and he is almost 4.

"What *do* Tiggers like?" he asked.

"Well," I said, "they don't like honey and they don't like haycorns and they don't like thistles. But they *do* like Roo's Strengthening Medicine, extract of malt."

"Tiggers like medicine?"

I nodded. "You can never tell about Tiggers."

I made a promise to myself to begin reading the Pooh books to Travis the next time he comes over. And he'll read them someday to someone else, and so ad infinitum.

They'll never get old.

It's like Milne said: "In that enchanted place on the top of the Forest, a little boy and his Bear will always be playing."

— 30 —

About Al Martinez

Al Martinez began writing essay columns of humor, observations and commentary for the Los Angeles Times in 1984, the year his profiles on three powerful Southern California Latinos helped bring a Pulitzer Prize to the Times for public service.

The columns first appeared in the Westside Section of the newspaper, then in the Valley Edition and are currently run three days a week in all editions of the 1.4-million circulation daily, one of the most respected and influential newspapers in the world.

In 1986, Martinez was voted among the top three essay columnists in America by the National Society of Newspaper Columnists.

In 1987, he won the prestigious National Headliner Award as the best columnist in the United States, an honor which, in the award's 54-year history, places him alongside other American writers such as Damon Runyon, Ernie Pyle, Edward R. Murrow, Heywood Broun, Stewart Alsop and Mike Royko.

Also in 1987, Martinez was named the best columnist in California by the California Newspaper Publishers Association.

Martinez has received a half-dozen other awards as well.

A native Californian, Martinez attended San Francisco State College, (now University), but left after three years to serve as a scout and then as a combat correspondent with the 7th Marine Regiment during the Korean War.

Upon discharge from the Marine Corps, he began his newspaper career as a general assignment reporter and feature writer with the Richmond Independent, a small Bay Area daily.

Continued on Next Page

Three years later, he moved to the Oakland Tribune, first as a reporter-feature writer and then as an essay columnist, writing social and political satire.

He wrote the column for the Oakland Tribune for eight years before joining the Los Angeles Times as a reporter and feature writer.

Martinez also writes movies and pilots for television and during a 10-year TV career has created three prime time network series. His latest movie, "That Secret Sunday" for CBS, won widespread critical acclaim.

He has also written two books, "Rising Voices," a series of profiles on Latinos, and "Jigsaw John," the story of a Los Angeles homicide detective that became a television series.

His short stories and profiles have appeared in magazines in the U.S. and abroad.

Martinez is married to the former Joanne Cinelli. They have a son, two daughters and three grandchildren. The Martinez family home is in the Santa Monica Mountain community of Topanga Canyon in Southern California.